W9-BPO-792

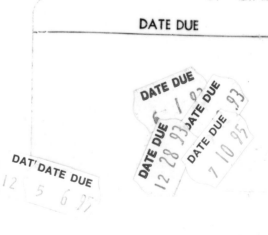

The Boy Who Could Do Anything

& Other Mexican Folk Tales

THE BOY

WHO COULD DO ANYTHING

& Other Mexican Folk Tales

Retold by Anita Brenner

Illustrated by Jean Charlot

Linnet Books • Hamden, Connecticut • 1992

First published 1942 by William R. Scott, Inc.
Revised edition published 1992 as a
Linnet Book, an imprint of
The Shoe String Press, Inc.
Hamden, Connecticut 06514.

Library of Congress Cataloging-in-Publication Data

Brenner, Anita, 1905–
The boy who could do anything and other Mexican folk tales /
retold by Anita Brenner : illustrated by Jean Charlot.
p.   cm.
Summary: Includes twenty-four Mexican folktales
dealing with ancient wisdom, everyday life, magic,
and the legendary character Tepozton.
1. Tales—Mexico. [1. Folklore—Mexico.]
I. Charlot, Jean, 1898–   ill.   II. Title.
PZ8.1.B74Bo 1992   93-3903   398.2′0972—dc20
ISBN 0-208-02353-4 (alk. paper)

The paper in this book meets the minimum requirements of
American National Standard for Information Sciences —
Permanence of Paper for Printed Library Materials, ANSI Z39.48 -1984. ∞

Printed in the United States of America

Table of Contents

STORY-TELLING IN MILPA ALTA

Luz, the Story-Teller

She is an Indian woman who lives in an Indian village in Mexico. Every night when the people come from the fields they tell each other stories.

Some are stories about things that happened in their own town, which is Milpa Alta. It means High Corn-Patch. Some are stories they make up. Some are things that the old people say were told to them by their grandfathers and they said it happened a long time ago, and that they heard it from their grandfathers.

Luz tells the best stories. She is a big comfortable woman and she likes to tell about Tepozton, the boy who could do anything, because these are the stories that everybody likes the best.

Luz knows more stories than anyone. She knows all kinds, and if you were an Indian and lived in Milpa Alta you could sit around the fire and hear her tell a different story every night until you were as old as your grandfather. But you would ask for some stories twice. Here they are.

6

The Boy Who Took Care of the Pigs

Juanito, the boy who took care of the pigs, was six years old. His father and mother were very poor. They all lived in a small house made of mud and stones. It had a straw roof. Inside, there was only one room and there was no floor. The ground was their floor. They cooked and they kept themselves warm with a fire which they made every day in the middle of the room. When they were sleepy they unrolled straw mats and put them down on the ground and covered themselves with old blankets and went to sleep on the mats. But sometimes they did not have enough wood for the fire and sometimes they did not have anything to cook. Juanito's father was sick. So the mother stayed to take care of him and Juanito got a job. His job was taking care of the pigs that belonged to a very rich man.

Every day Juanito took the pigs out in the woods and while they grunted and snuffled around looking for acorns, Juanito picked up all the good pieces of fire-wood that he could find. And in the evening he would say to the rich man, "Master, the pigs are asleep and the day is over. Will you give me permission to take this wood to my father so he can keep warm?"

People would see him every day gathering up wood and every evening carrying it on his back to his father and they would say, "Juanito is a very good boy. He deserves to have luck. If we wish hard enough and long enough something nice must surely happen."

One day the rich man moved far away to his ranch and the pigs went too, so Juanito had to go and take care of them. He said, "I wonder how I can take wood to my father every night? It is so far, but I must do it somehow."

So every evening he asked for permission and he would walk and walk and walk until he got home with the fire-wood. It was dark. Then when he went back to the ranch it was still darker and cold but Juanito was so happy that he could take wood to his father that he did not feel so cold.

Every day seemed just the same but this day it was different. Juanito saw the pigs snuffling and grunting and digging into the ground with their feet and their snouts, and he saw them pulling things out of the ground that looked like nice thick wood. He picked one piece up and it was very heavy. He said, "How wonderful. This will burn a long time."

The pieces were all the same size so he made a bundle easily but when it was time to take the bundle home it seemed very heavy. Juanito was so happy to have such good wood that somehow he got this bundle home and he did not feel too tired.

His father said, "Listen, my son, where did you get this?"

The boy answered, "Dear Father, the pigs dug it up out of the earth. I hope it will make you very warm."

The father said, "There is something very funny about these sticks. If the master sees them maybe he will want them. Maybe he will take your job away and go out in the woods with the pigs himself and gather up these sticks himself."

Juanito laughed. "Oh Father, why should the master go out in the woods if he can hire me to do it for him?"

So every day Juanito came home with a bundle of these strange heavy sticks and his master did not notice how strange they were.

What could they be? Juanito did not know but his father did. They were pure silver that some bandits had hidden away in the ground. Should he tell anybody? No, he was old and poor and sick. They would take it away from him. So he just kept it and he said, "When Juanito grows up he will know what to do with this."

Juanito took care of the pigs for ten years and all this time the silver he was bringing home was piling up all around the inside of the house until it was like a wall around the room. "How nice," he said. "This extra wall certainly keeps the room much warmer."

But one day he came home with a very sad face and he said, "Dear Father, the master has sold all the pigs and I do not have a job any more. What are we going to do?"

His father was a very very old man now and he just smiled and said, "You come with me."

They took one of the pieces to the place where the government makes money and there it was cut into round silver coins. They did this every day until they had a sack full of money and then they just stood and looked at it and laughed and said, "Ha, ha, now we are rich."

After a while the master came looking for Juanito to tell him that now he had some more pigs and please come and take care of them. But he could not find the house because where it had been, there was now a very elegant pink house and it had roses growing all around it. He knocked at the door and said to the lady, "Madam, can you tell me where to find Juanito, the pig boy?"

"Enter, enter sir, he is not a boy any more. He has grown up but he is still Juanito."

The master came in and he was astonished. They took him into the dining-room and there was a big table with wonderful things to eat on it and many people sitting around it having a very good time eating all they wanted to. The master said, "What an elegant house! What rich furniture! What fine food! And what beautiful silver dishes! Did you get all this working for me?"

Juanito was sitting at the head of the table carving a ham and a turkey and six chickens for the people he had invited. They were all the poorest people in the town.

He said, "Master, will you join us in a little bit of supper? Just what we have, of course, not so fine as you are accustomed to, but we would be happy to have you share our poor meal."

"Thank you, thank you, Juanito. I will be glad to have some of this wonderful supper but please first answer my question. How could you get all this working for me?"

Juanito smiled and said, "Well, you see I worked so long."

And everybody laughed and said, "Well you see we wished so hard."

The master wondered why they were laughing, but he never found out.

The Happy Milkmaid

This was a maid named Josephine. She worked in a rich house. There they gave her all the milk that was left over. This family was so rich that the milk they bought in the morning was not used at night, so what was left over in the morning they gave to Josephine. And what was left over in the evening they gave her too.

Josephine made the best of it. She went out every day to market to sell the milk that they gave her. One day they gave her more milk than ever. She was so happy she was dancing with joy on her way to the market. She would think about something and suddenly she would skip and jump. Her mind was far away. She did not remember she was carrying milk.

She was thinking about all the things she would do with the money she would get for the milk. First she would buy a hen and this hen would lay many eggs. Many eggs. She would sell the eggs and with that money she would buy a pig. In her mad imagination she thought of the many ways she could fatten the pig. She could just see him swelling up and getting bigger and bigger.

12

She was saying to herself, "When I sell those eggs I will buy that pig and I will give him barley and acorns and then when he is big and fat I shall sell him and buy a calf—no, two calves, and they will grow and get bigger and bigger and soon they will be cows and I shall have milk from my own cows and what will I do with it? I will take it all to market and sell it! I will be selling the milk from my own cows."

She thought of herself in the market with all the milk and this made her so happy that she skipped with joy. And she tripped and fell with her jug of milk and then, oh then all her dreams came to nothing. Every intention she had was finished. She sat down right in the street and cried. And she said over and over, "Good-by hen, eggs, pig, and cows! Good-by hen, good-by eggs, good-by pig and good-by cows."

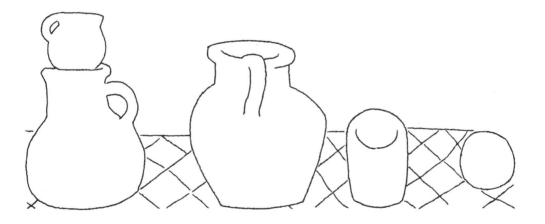

Dumb Juan and the Bandits

There was a house with three sons. The mother was a very old lady. She got sick. The eldest brother had to go out to work and the youngest went to buy medicines for his mother, while Juan stayed in the house to take care of her. They called him Dumb Juan because he was stupid.

They said, "Heat some water for a bath." Their mother wanted a bath. They were going to help her when they got home. But Juan was very stupid. He made the water too hot, it was boiling. He put his mother in and was very pleased. She opened her mouth and waved her hands and screamed.

His brothers were coming home and they heard her screaming and they ran. Juan said, "Look, I am giving Mother a bath and see how happy she is." He thought she was laughing but no, she was making terrible faces because the water was too hot.

"What a dumb Juan!" said the brothers, and they took her out gently. And then she was even sicker than she was before.

So now the youngest son had to stay home and cook, and every day the eldest son went out to work. But Juan, who was the middle one, didn't do anything. They didn't let him because he always did everything wrong.

One day the youngest one said to the oldest one, "I'm getting very tired of having that dumb Juan around the house. He gets in my way and breaks things. I think we ought to take him out in the woods and lose him."

"All right," said the older brother. "Let's start off and pretend we don't want to take him. Then he will be sure to follow." So they

14

started out and they went a long way and Juan kept right on following after them.

At last the brothers said, "What are you doing here, Juan? We didn't say you could come along. Go home now and get the dog."

So Juan started back through the woods. The youngest brother said to the oldest one, "Such a stupid Juan. Now he will surely get lost." And they went on.

But Juan knew his way through the woods and when he got home, the first thing he did was to take the *door* off its hinges. He put it on his back and he started back through the woods. Instead of getting the dog, he was getting the door.

Pretty soon his brothers saw him coming through the woods carrying the door. They scolded him. They said, "What are you doing with that, you stupid boy?"

He said, "I am bringing the door."

They said, "We told you to get the dog, not the door."

"Well, here it is," said Juan.

"Oh, what a stupid boy! Now you will have to carry it all the way into the mountains." So they went on, and suddenly they heard a terrible noise. It was the sound of galloping horses. It was a gang of robbers coming back from having robbed.

The two brothers scrambled up a big tree that had very thick branches so no one could see them. Dumb Juan went up too. Then they saw the first bandit come galloping up, and he shouted, "Here is a good place!"

The others came and they all got off their horses and sat down under the tree. They made a fire and started cooking supper.

Pretty soon Juan said, "Oh, brothers, this dog has tired me very much."

"That's not a dog, it's the door. And who told you to bring it up in the tree, anyway? Such a stupid Juan. Be quiet. If the bandits hear us they will kill us."

A little while later Juan said, "Brothers, if this dog doesn't stop tickling me I think I am going to have to laugh!"

"What a stupid Juan! How can that door tickle you?"

"I don't know, but this is a tickling dog and it's tickling me. Besides, my nose itches and I am going to sneeze and I have to blow it and how can I blow my nose while I am holding this dog?"

"Be quiet," said the brothers, "do you want to get killed?"

Juan held the door with one hand and tried to blow his nose at the same time, but the door almost fell out of the tree.

The bandits heard the rustling up in the tree and they were very frightened. "Who is hiding up there?" one of them said.

"Oh, it must be a bird, it must be a bird," said another. So they went on eating their supper.

A little later Juan said, "Brothers, I am getting very sleepy. How can I go to sleep in a tree?"

"Be quiet," whispered the two brothers very angrily.

Juan said, "If I don't talk I will go to sleep and then I will drop this dog right on the bandits."

"If you keep on talking we will all get killed. Can't you understand anything?"

"Well if I can't talk, then can I sing?" said Juan.

"Oh, it's no use! You can do anything you want to and if you get killed it will be your own fault."

So Juan began to sing and the bandits heard him. "Oh, it must be that bird again," they said. So they went on eating their supper.

Then Juan said, "I just can't stand it any more. I am going to drop this dog." And he did.

It made an awful noise and when the bandits heard the crash, they yelled, "It must be other bandits who are stronger than we are and who have been waiting for us!" They saddled their horses and mules as fast as they could and they went off in a hurry.

Juan came sliding down the tree very fast and he found a bag of gold they had left behind. Then he saw a horse that they had not had time to saddle. So he took the bag of gold and he climbed on the horse and he went galloping away.

From that time on he was a very rich man, so nobody called him Dumb Juan any more.

The Ant, the Lamb, the Cricket, & the Mouse

This was a lovely little ant, sweeping in front of her little house. And sweeping, sweeping, she found a golden penny. She began to think about what she could do with that money.

She said, "If I lend money at interest that would turn out well, but what I am afraid of is that my friends would come asking me for things, and if I start a store the locusts would come and eat all the grain. The best thing is to buy a beautiful hat and a lovely dress and make myself pretty and see if that way somebody loves me. Then maybe I will get married."

She bought everything she had thought of, as well as a beautiful and luxurious mirror. When she had everything she wanted, she dressed up and she held up her beautiful mirror and looked at her beautiful self. She said, "Now I am ready," and she went out on the street wearing all her new things.

As she went along, she met some very nice looking lambs, and she said to the nicest one, "Dear little lamb, will you do me the very great favor of telling me how I look?"

He said, "Why you look very nice, my dear little ant."

"Oh, well, do you know I would like to get married and this is why I have dressed up? Wouldn't you like to marry me?"

"If you like," said the lamb, "we will get married."

"Very well," said the ant. "But let's see first, how are you going to talk to me?"

"Oh," said the lamb. "Beh, beh, beh."

"No, no," said the ant. "If you talk to me like that I shall be frightened. After all, I don't love you, my dear little lamb. You can go now."

Just then a cricket was passing by and the ant told him she wanted to get married.

"You look so nice," said the cricket, "I will certainly marry you."

"All right," said the ant, "but first I want to know how you are going to talk to me."

The cricket answered, "Gree, gree, gree."

Said the ant, "I don't like your way of talking. It would frighten me. So good-by, little cricket, you can skip along."

Now a very pretty little mouse came by, very nicely dressed. And the ant said, "Dear little mouse, my idea is that I want to get married but I have not yet succeeded in my plan. I think I will decide to marry you, dear little mouse."

"All right, little ant, I accept with pleasure," he said.

"Very well, little mouse, but I want to know first how you are going to talk to me."

"So you want to know how I am going to talk to you? Very well, I am going to say, listen; 'Eeee, eeee, eeee.' "

"Well, that might frighten me," said the ant. "It might, but anyway let us get married, dear little mouse."

So they got married and they were very happy. Some days, the little ant would say to the little mouse, "I want you to go to the market for me, to buy all our groceries."

And he would answer, "No, I can't go. You go, and I will stay home and cook."

The ant accepted this arrangement and would go to market, but first she would tell the mouse what to cook and when to put vegetables in the soup. And then the little ant would go to the market thinking how much she loved her little mouse.

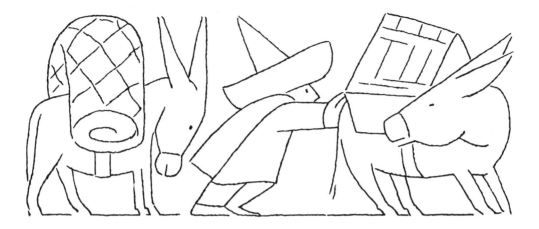

Some Impatient Mule-Drivers

Once some mule-drivers were on their way to a fair with sponges and hot chili peppers, which they were going to sell. The mules that carried sponges went much faster because sponges are light. "That's fine," said their drivers. "We will get in first and sell everything quickly. Hurry up, hurry up!"

The mules that were carrying chili didn't go so fast. "Mules are stubborn," said one driver, "but I have an idea." He took some chili and rubbed it on the legs of the slow mules. It burned their legs and they began to run. They ran so fast that they left all the other animals behind.

"You certainly are clever," said the other mule-drivers. "You will be famous some day." So the impatient mule-drivers rubbed chili on all the mules. Off they went. The drivers couldn't keep up with them. The mules ran into a river and splashed in and came whiffing out on the other side.

Now their legs didn't burn any more. The water had washed all the chili off. The drivers found them standing on the river-bank resting, but the water had swelled the sponges. They were so large that everybody at the fair bought some. They looked much better than the little sponges that the other drivers brought. The impatient mule-drivers thought they were very clever. "It takes brains to succeed in this world," they said.

With the money they got, the impatient mule-drivers bought big bags of salt. "We will take this to another fair very fast and make a lot more money," they said. And they rubbed chili on the legs of the mules the minute they started. Salt is heavy but the mules ran very fast because their legs burned so. They ran and ran until they came to a deep river and then they stampeded in so fast that their feet hardly touched the bottom. They snorted and snuffled and plunged around in the water until all the chili was washed off. But when they came out the other side, they had no packs left. For the water had washed away all the salt. It was gone.

The mules felt so light and cool that when the drivers found them, they couldn't catch them. They ran and ran, but the animals just pranced around. From time to time they tossed their heads and brayed cheerfully. "Awh-eee-awh!" Then they galloped away, but far off they could be heard, "Awh-eee-awh-eee-awh!"

The mule-drivers sat on the ground and cried. They had lost their salt, their money, and their mules. Which just shows that people who think they are clever are sometimes mistaken.

Teutli, the Mountain That Is Alive

That mountain named Teutli is really a man. He is enchanted there. Some say he is the Emperor Moctezuma, waiting for the day when all the Indians will be masters of their land again. Many engineers have gone there to see, because sometimes the mountain makes a noise. It roars and grumbles. The engineers say it is only because he is a volcano, but they don't know everything.

Old Teutli has a rock of gold. Pure gold. Some people have tried to steal it, but old Teutli does not allow it. Two engineers went there and one of them started to dig and he fell off and broke into little pieces. The other one did not want to dig, so he was saved and came back and told the story. Teutli is bad.

They say that Teutli, old, old Teutli had a daughter. She was named White Lady, that is Malintzin. White Lady. This lovely girl wanted to marry a young man who was very handsome but her father did not want to let her go. So instead he turned them both into mountains. One is the white one, they call it Sleeping Lady now. The other one has fire in it and gives off smoke, so it is the Smoking Mountain.

The old Teutli also enchanted a shepherd and all his sheep right next to the white mountain because this poor shepherd went to see Teutli to ask him to please let the girl marry. There they are at the foot of the mountain, together with an enchanted archbishop, they are all taking care of Teutli's daughter so that nobody shall touch her. Old Teutli loved her so much that he could not let her marry, so he made her into a mountain and covered her with snow and nobody can come near.

Teutli takes care of the people of Milpa Alta. He does not like to

23

see anybody come and mistreat anybody in his town, and when people come to Milpa Alta with such intentions he sends lightning and there they are, finished.

Seventeen years ago in the time of the revolution on a day when the town was getting ready to celebrate its big holiday and everybody was going to enjoy himself, some soldiers came, sent by the government. They intended to climb down into Milpa Alta and do much damage. They were killing people wherever they went and breaking into houses and stealing everything. But they could not do that to Milpa Alta, old Teutli would not allow it.

The soldiers just did one thing. They shot off three machine-guns and two cannons. This was about four o'clock in the afternoon and the sun was shining. Old Teutli grew dark, a great shower came down and then there was one bolt of lightning. It killed every soldier in that camp instantly. The camp was empty, there wasn't a single soldier left.

Teutli. Old Teutli does not like strangers. He hates the city people and he hates foreigners and he does not want any strangers around doing wicked things to the people. That is why Milpa Alta has no water. Old Teutli prefers to have his town suffer rather than have strangers coming around. One day in the dry season some strangers came. They came from a town where there are many powerful wizards. They arrived in Milpa Alta and asked for water and the people said, "There is none, there is none."

"What do you mean, there is no water? Of course there is water," and they lifted a rock and out came water.

All the people filled their jugs at this spring and then the men covered it up and said, "Do you want water all the time? Give us four people, two women and two men. We will give you all the water you will ever need if you give us those four people, but they

25

have to be good people, the ones with the biggest warmest hearts in town."

"No, no," everybody said. "We would not turn anybody over to you, we are all friends here. We do not want to see anybody disappear or be bewitched or something."

So the water dried up and the men went away. They went off in the direction of old Teutli. And they disappeared. A bolt of lightning came down and they were finished. So Milpa Alta still has no water and when anybody needs water he has to go a long way to get it. For they did not wish to see anybody hurt.

Old Teutli does not want trains to come. If trains come old Teutli is going to explode because that is his arrangement. The only water there is comes from his land. It is the only spring. If trains come, the spring will dry up, there will not be a drop. Teutli does not want trains because he does not like the noise, and old Teutli, he does not want trains because he does not care to see anybody run over. Teutli: what is bad about him, is good about him too. Old Teutli.

THE BOY WHO COULD DO ANYTHING

Tepozton

A long time ago there was a little boy and his name was Tepozton. In a way, he was just like other children and in a way he was not. But it was not known he had magic powers until he was seven years old.

Tepozton lived in a little house next to a river. It belonged to two old people and the little boy thought they were his father and mother, but they really were not. His real father was a god who lived above the clouds on top of a very high mountain that had fire inside. It was called a volcano and he lived up there above the volcano with all the other gods.

They had jobs to do. It was their business to make the rain fall at the right time so that the plants would grow. They also trimmed the winds to keep them from getting too rough. They experimented with many things and when they found how to do anything useful they would teach it to the people. They taught them how to weave cloth and how to make dishes and build houses and dig mines, and they showed them how to take rubber out of the trees to make balls so that they could play games and have a lot of fun.

In their spare time, the gods amused themselves by riding around in the clouds or else they would turn themselves into all kinds of animals to see what it felt like. They also liked to watch the silly things that the people on earth were doing. But their main amusement was playing ball. They had big ball games and they would bet whole mountains on them. When they were tired they sat down to smoke out of long clay pipes. That was how it happened that the Indians were the first people in the world who learned what tobacco was because, after all, these were Indian gods.

Now the god who was Tepozton's real father got tired one day of watching the balls bounce and of riding around in the clouds. He smoked so much that his head ached but still he was not having a good time any more.

His best friend could not understand it. All the other gods were still enjoying themselves. "I don't see why you should be any different," he said. "What is good enough for us ought to be good enough for you!"

"I know," said the tired god, "but I guess I must be different. You know what I would like? I would like to have a little boy. I am sure I never would get tired of him."

"Nonsense," said his friend. "Who ever heard of a god having a little boy? Besides, little boys are just a lot of fuss and bother. And it is too cold up here for little children anyway."

"I am afraid it is," sighed the poor unhappy god, "but still, I

29

would like to have a little boy. Even if I could not keep him here with me. I think I will go down to earth and see about it."

"Stuff and nonsense!" said the other god.

But the unhappy god slid down the mountain and started walking around on the earth. Of course, nobody knew who he was. He was dressed just like anybody else. One day he stopped at a spring to get a drink of water. While he was there a beautiful girl came to fill her pitcher at the spring. He fell in love with her and she fell in love with him, so they went away together and after a while they had a little boy. The god was very happy. At last his wish had come true.

But he was very sad also because he couldn't stay down on earth any longer. He had to go back to the mountain and help regulate the rain and look after the crops. If he didn't do it the people on earth would not have enough to eat. And even his own little boy would go hungry. So he said good-by and disappeared. When the girl looked at the place where he had been standing, she saw a small green stone, as green as a growing plant. It was round and smooth. She made a hole in it and hung it around the baby's neck.

That baby was Tepozton. She took him home but her father and mother were angry. They wanted to kill him. They said, "Where is his father? A child without a father has no business being born at all!"

What could she say? She said, "He is a beautiful baby."

"It doesn't matter how beautiful he is. He has to die. We don't understand why, nobody does. That's just the way things are."

So she went far out in the fields but she couldn't bear to hurt the baby. She walked and walked and it grew dark and still she did not know what to do. At last she put him down very gently in the center

30

of a big plant, a maguey plant, which has big broad leaves growing around it. She put the baby down and ran away crying.

Then she went home and told her father and mother what she had done. "That's right," they said. "The baby will die of hunger and cold." But the girl cried and cried.

The next day she slipped out and went to see what had happened to the baby. She saw the plant all curled up, the nice broad leaves were over the baby to keep him warm. He was fast asleep and rosy. There was a little hole in one of the leaves and something like milk was dripping out of it and falling into the baby's mouth. The girl tasted it. It was warm and sweet.

She played with her baby for a while, but then it grew late and she knew she had to do something, or her father and mother would be very angry. So she laid the baby down in the middle of an ant-hill. "Oh dear, oh dear, now he will surely die, the ants will kill him," and she went home crying.

But the next day when she came back she saw the baby all covered up with pink rose petals and he was kicking and gurgling. The ants were bringing more and more petals, and other ants were bringing honey and putting it down carefully on the baby's lips. So the girl was frightened. "If my father and mother find out the baby is still alive, they will punish me terribly," she said. So she put the baby in a wooden box, and nailed the cover down tightly, and put it in the river. And the river carried the box away.

Now, down near the mouth of the river there lived an old fisherman and his wife. They were very happy but they wanted children to play with. When the old fisherman saw the box bobbing up and down in the water he waded in after it quickly, and then ran home to his wife saying, "Look what I found!"

She was very suspicious until she opened the box. But when she saw what was inside she danced with joy. "Oh, at last we have a little baby, a little son!" She made him some clothes at once, and even some little sandals for his feet. "What shall we name him?"

Her husband said, "He has a green stone, a mountain stone, around his neck. Let us call him Tepozton, the Mountain Boy," he suggested.

"Oh, what a pretty name, Tepozton, Tepoztin, Tepoztitzin! It makes nice nicknames, too!" So it was decided.

The little boy grew up strong and happy with his adopted parents, who loved him very much. When he was seven years old the old fisherman made him a little bow and some little arrows for it.

"Now you don't have to fish or hunt any more, Papa," Tepozton said. "I shall bring home everything we need."

"Ha, ha!" laughed the old man. "You're just seven years old and your bow isn't big enough to kill a fly! What do you expect to bring home for dinner?"

"I can shoot anything at all," said Tepozton. "Just anything at all."

"All right, there's a quail over there. Shoot it," said the old man.

Tepozton fitted an arrow to his bow and shot. The funny thing was that he shot straight up into the air, but the quail fell dead anyhow.

"That's strange," said the old man. "But maybe it just happened. There's a wild turkey over there on that tree. Shoot it," he said, but he thought to himself that even a big man with a big bow could never hit that turkey. It was too far away. And yet when Tepozton fitted an arrow to his bow, and again shot straight into the air, the turkey fell out of the tree, dead.

After that Tepozton got everything that was needed with his

little bow and arrows. He went out every day at six o'clock in the morning and did not come back until six o'clock in the afternoon. He walked so much and so far that he wore out many pairs of sandals. One day the old fisherman's wife said to him, "Tepozton, what do you do all day in the mountains?"

"Oh," said the strange little boy, "I have many things to attend to."

She did not ask any more questions but she thought it all very queer. Of course she did not know that Tepozton had magic powers, but she suspected something just the same. And pretty soon everybody found out that he was not an ordinary person. This was when he had a very big adventure with a man-eating giant.

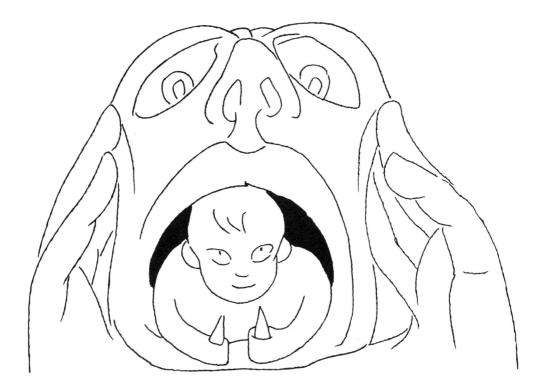

How Tepozton Killed the Giant

There were tigers and wolves and lions in the woods where Tepozton went hunting. But he was not afraid. Sometimes he would come around a bend in the trail and right in front of him there would be a big wolf. Tepozton would stand very still and look at the animal, and the beast would look at him out of his burning eyes. And Tepozton would say, "Eh, little brother, get out of my way please, I have many things to attend to." And the wolf would go quietly away.

So he was not afraid either when he heard about the wicked man-eating giant. This giant had to be fed a live human being every

34

year in the spring. The people who lived near him had to choose somebody to be eaten by the giant because if they didn't, the giant would go out and kill many, many of them. They had made an agreement with him not to do that, if they themselves brought somebody for his pot. And he agreed because he was a lazy giant.

Each year it was a different town, and the families in each town took turns. When Tepozton was seven years old it was the fisherman's turn to feed the giant. He had nobody but himself and his wife and Tepozton, so of course he decided to go himself. He didn't say anything about it but when the soldiers came to get him, Tepozton knew what they were there for.

"No indeed," said Tepozton to the soldiers, "I will not allow you to take him. He is old anyhow and I am young, and the giant will be pleased to have a tender morsel." He begged and begged the old fisherman and told him that nothing could happen to him. Finally the fisherman believed him and told him he could go.

Before he started out, Tepozton built a little fire in the corner of the yard. "Watch this fire," he said. "When the smoke is white, that means I am safe. But if it turns grey, I am in danger. And if it is black, it means I am dead." Then he said good-by and went away with the soldiers.

As Tepozton walked along the road he picked up little pieces of black glass. This glass had been thrown up by the volcano where the gods lived. The people made arrow-heads out of it. It was as sharp as a razor blade and it was a beautiful shiny black. Little Tepozton filled his pockets with it. The soldiers didn't notice. They thought it was just a game.

At last they came to the palace of the man-eating giant. When he saw Tepozton he shouted, "How do you expect me to make a meal off that little shrimp?"

35

"That was all there was, Your Majesty," said the poor soldiers.

"I'm little but I taste good, Your Majesty," said Tepozton. "You just try me. All good things come in small packages." But the giant only roared.

Then the soldiers put Tepozton in a big black pot full of boiling water. They put the lid on. Tepozton didn't make a sound. The giant lay down and took a nap while he waited for his dinner to cook.

Pretty soon he woke up and roared, "I'm getting very hungry!" He took the lid off the pot and looked in to see how his dinner was getting along. But instead of a tender little boy, what do you think he saw? He saw a great big spotted tiger. It opened its mouth and roared even louder than the giant, so loud it made him jump. So he put the lid back very fast and decided to wait some more.

Soon he woke up again, hungrier than ever. This time the giant took the lid off very carefully and what do you think he saw? He saw a huge snake. It was coiled round and round inside the pot and when the giant looked in, the snake hissed at him. So he put the lid back again and fell asleep.

But the next time he woke up he was so hungry he didn't care what he ate. He rushed over to the pot, grabbed the lid, and there was the little boy inside, laughing at him! The giant let out a fierce roar, and although Tepozton wasn't cooked at all, he took him by the seat of his pants and popped him right into his enormous mouth. And when that happened, the fire that Tepozton had made in the yard of the fisherman's house suddenly turned dark grey.

"Oh, dear," the old man said. "I knew I should have gone myself!" And the old woman began to cry.

But Tepozton scrambled down the giant's throat and didn't give him a chance to chew. When he got down to his stomach he put his hand in his pocket and took out one of the little pieces of glass. He began to cut and cut and cut.

Soon he wore out one piece of glass. He took another out of his pocket and kept on cutting. Before long he had made a large hole in the giant's stomach.

"Oh, my," howled the giant. "I have a dreadful bellyache!" But Tepozton went right on cutting.

"Oh, my!" howled the giant. "Get a doctor quick! I'm poisoned!" By this time the hole was very large. It was so large that a little daylight was beginning to come in.

Suddenly Tepozton cut right through to the outside. The giant screamed dreadfully and a doctor came running. But it was too late. The giant was dead, and Tepozton climbed out and shook hands with everybody. And the smoke of the fisherman's fire turned white as snow.

Tepozton lived in the giant's house after that and was crowned king instead. He taught the people many things. In his spare time he amused himself by playing ball, and riding in the clouds, and turning into all kinds of animals. But most of all, he enjoyed walking around dressed like a poor and ordinary person. In that way he could find out what was going on and help the people who needed help. Some people say that now he lives on the mountain with the gods, and others say no, he lives on earth and is always helping people. But it is hard to tell because he looks just like an ordinary person.

How Tepozton Hung the Bells

When Tepozton killed the giant he became very famous. He was so famous that even the people in the city heard about him. The rich and mighty gentlemen who lived there wanted to meet him and were always inviting him to dinner. But he always refused, and this made him more famous than ever.

These people who lived in the city thought that big buildings were very wonderful. The bigger they were the more they admired them, and they admired themselves especially for building them. But they were never happy because they were afraid that some other city would build still bigger ones. So they decided to build the biggest and highest one in the world, and it would be a church.

First they sent their engineers to measure all the buildings in the world. They wanted to make sure that theirs would be the biggest one of all. It took a long time for the engineers to do all this measuring, and they got very tired climbing stairs and riding elevators. But at last they got home with all the measurements and began to build a church that would be twice as big and twice as high as the biggest of all the big buildings in the world.

When Tepozton heard about this he laughed and laughed. "As for me," he said, "I like to be up high, too. That is why I live on top of a mountain. When I get tired of this one I'll move to another one, maybe a higher one." And he laughed and laughed.

It took a great deal of money to build the biggest church in the world. The city people were very proud of that. But when it was all finished, they heard that another city was building a bigger one. It was two feet higher than theirs. This made them terribly angry. Tepozton laughed very hard when he heard about it.

The people in the city wanted to go to war with the other city that was building a church two feet higher than theirs, but the chief engineer said, "No, we don't have to go to war about it! You just watch me! I'll show them!" And immediately he added a high steeple to the church. Everybody was very proud and happy. "Now we have the highest building of all," they said.

They planned to celebrate with a big parade. The bells in the steeple would ring all day long. Everybody would dress up in his best clothes. They would all shake hands with each other. But when the bells arrived, nobody could hang them in the steeple. It was too high. Even the engineer could not think of what to do about it.

The people were so angry they wanted to hang the engineer. But

39

he was a clever man. "Wait!" he said. "Let's get Tepozton. I have heard he can do anything. Maybe he can hang our bells."

"Pooh!" they said. "He's just a boy. He's just a country upstart. What does he know about steeples?"

The engineer felt that way himself but he did not want to be hanged, so he appointed a committee to go with him and see Tepozton.

"So you want me to hang the bells in your church steeple," said Tepozton to the engineer and his committee. "Well, I can do it, I guess. Only I don't feel like taking that long trip to the city. Besides, I don't like the city. It's hot and dirty, and there are too many people in it."

"But we'll pay you for your trouble!" cried the engineer. "We might even pay you ten thousand pieces of silver!"

Tepozton laughed. "I don't need any silver," he said. "But I'll tell you what I'll do. I have heard that you have very nice pigeons in the city. I think I would like to have some of those. They are very pretty. If you give me fifty pigeons I will hang the bells for you."

"All right," said the engineer. "We will give you fifty pigeons, on the condition that you hang the bells at once. You see, we have planned a parade. It is supposed to be next Sunday and if the bells aren't up we can't have it. Besides, they might hang me instead."

"I'll come on Sunday morning and do it," said Tepozton.

"Oh, but that won't be soon enough! The steeple is so high it might take you a week!"

"Do you think so?" said Tepozton. "All right, then get somebody else to do it. I am very busy watching the corn grow and the clouds take different shapes."

Of course, they had to agree to let him do it whenever he wanted to. But they said that if the bells were not ready to ring by the time of the parade, they would surely hang the engineer. Tepozton told him not to worry, everything would be all right.

Early Sunday morning everybody crowded to the windows to watch Tepozton come to town. They thought it was very funny that a boy from the country should try to do what an important engineer couldn't do. "It's because he is so ignorant," they said.

While they were talking, Tepozton arrived. But they didn't notice because he was dressed like a poor boy. They thought surely he would ride into town in a golden coach. After all he was supposed to be a king.

There he was, standing at the foot of the church looking up at the steeple, dressed like an ordinary person. Everybody began to laugh. They were all out on the roofs of the buildings, and in the windows, laughing and watching Tepozton to see what he would do now.

Suddenly the wind began to blow. It blew and blew, and the people had to rush inside to keep from being blown away. Then they heard the sound of bells and the wind stopped. They went out quickly—and the bells were in the steeple! Tepozton was still standing on the ground looking up, and he was laughing. They begged him to tell how he did it, but he would not.

"Please give me my pigeons now," he said. "I must go home to my mountain."

"But won't you stay for the parade? There are going to be many people in it."

"No thank you. I have to go and see how many different colors my white flowers are."

"What a silly thing to say!" they remarked. "He must be crazy!"

"Maybe he is very wise," others declared. "That is why we don't understand what he says."

41

"But he doesn't use any long words! Why shouldn't we understand him?"

While they were arguing, Tepozton took his pigeons and left. They were in a big box. Eight men went along to carry it. Tepozton went ahead to show them the road. When he was far ahead, the men started to talk. They said, "It's impossible that this box should have only pigeons in it. It is too heavy. There must be something valuable inside. Who ever heard of anybody who would take fifty pigeons instead of ten thousand pieces of silver?"

So they opened the box. And the pigeons all flew out. Tepozton was so angry that he turned the men to stone and they are still standing where he left them. Ever since that time, he has never gone to the city again.

The Magic Grocery Store

Once there was a man who was very poor. He was hungry but there was nothing to eat in the house. It was a holiday too, New Year's Eve. His wife scolded him because they were so poor. Sadly he went out to his cornfield.

44

The cornfield was dry. It was growing dark, and as the sun went down the leaves began to whisper together. "Poor, poor, poor," they rustled, "poor, poor." Then the wind began to blow. It blew harder and harder until it was a whirlwind, catching up leaves and dust and whirling them round and round. Back and forth over the field whirled the wind, faster and faster.

All of a sudden the whirlwind stopped in front of the poor man, who was named Manuel. Something stepped out of the dust and leaves. It was a young man. "Do you know who I am?" he said to Manuel.

"I think I do," said Manuel. "I think you must be Tepozton. You look like an ordinary person but you ride in the wind."

"Yes. That is who I am. I am going to help you. Step right into my whirlwind, Manuel."

Manuel stepped in, and instead of dust and leaves he saw something like a small round room. It was made of many colors and there was a comfortable place to sit. Tepozton sat next to him and they whirled away.

When they stopped, they were at the foot of a mountain. Manuel thought he recognized it. He thought it was the mountain where Tepozton lived. He could see the top, very far away, from his own house. But here they were right at the foot of it.

As they were standing there, a door opened. It opened out of the mountain. Light streamed from it. Manuel saw many people moving around inside. Other people were coming up a path and going in.

"It's a magic grocery store," said Tepozton. "It belongs to me. Here are twenty-five cents. Go in and buy anything you want. You can get everything you need for twenty-five cents. But I warn you, it is now eleven o'clock. At twelve the door closes and it does not open

again until next New Year. If you take too long, you will be shut up inside of the mountain for a whole year."

Manuel hesitated because he was afraid. Tepozton said, "Don't you believe it is a magic store? Look at me . . ." and he began to turn into a handsome elegant young man, all dressed in colored feathers and precious stones. Then he turned into a tiger, and then into a big spotted snake. And as quickly as that, there he was again just an ordinary person. "Now do you believe me?" he said.

So Manuel thanked him and went into the store. It was a store just like any other. There were three clerks waiting on the people. Manuel bought some beans, some peppers, a little cheese, and some bread. The clerks put them in a bag and he went away.

When Manuel got home his wife was already asleep. He laid the bag down beside her and went to sleep too.

But the next morning, when he woke up and opened the bag, there weren't any beans inside. None of the things Manuel had bought were there. The bag was full of gold. Manuel was rich. Now he and his wife always had something for dinner. So of course she did not scold him again.

The Man Who Stayed Too Long

Manuel and his wife were sitting down to a fine New Year's Eve dinner when somebody knocked at the door. He went to open it and it was a friend named Pedro. Pedro said, "I am so poor and hungry."

"Sit right down and have some dinner with us," said Manuel, "and then I will show you something wonderful. I invite you to go to a magic place with me."

"But I have to tell my wife," said Pedro. "Otherwise she might worry about me."

"All right, just tell her you are going out with me. I will come to your house for you."

Manuel and Pedro started at ten o'clock. They went very fast, and when they got to the magic store it was already eleven. Many people were inside and the clerks were very busy. Manuel said, "Here are twenty-five cents. You can get anything in the store for that. But I warn you that it means you must hurry. If you do not leave before twelve, you will be shut up in the mountain for a whole year."

48

Pedro went in. He liked the store so much that he just looked and looked, and kept on buying more and more groceries. He was greedy. He did not notice how late it was getting because he wanted so many things.

The next morning Pedro's wife came to see Manuel. "Where is my husband?" she asked him.

"Isn't he home?" said Manuel.

"No indeed, he is not home. You took him away, and now you are responsible. If you do not bring him back I shall call the police."

"But I can't bring him back," said Manuel. "I told him to leave that place before twelve. Now he must be shut up inside."

Pedro's wife was very angry and she went to see the judge and demanded that Manuel be made to bring back her husband. The judge called Manuel and said that if he did not bring Pedro back he would be punished. Maybe he would be shot. Manuel explained how everything had happened, and the judge decided to wait for a year. If Pedro did not come back next New Year's, then Manuel would be shot.

This arrangement was written down, and everybody signed it; Manuel should bring back Pedro in the same condition as he had taken him.

So when New Year's came around again, Manuel went straight to the mountain. The store was open but he was afraid to go in. He stood at the door and watched. Pretty soon he saw Pedro come by the door. He grabbed him quickly by the arm and pulled him out. "What were you doing in there such a long time?" he said. "Aren't you ashamed of yourself staying away for a whole year? Don't you ever get enough?"

"Why, I've been here only a short time," said Pedro. He had been a whole year in the mountain and still he said it was only a short time! He didn't even know it was a year. That is how magic things work.

Next day Manuel delivered Pedro to the judge. Four doctors were called in to examine him, to see if he was in the same condition as when he left. And he was. He did not have the slightest mark of any kind. So they sent him back to his wife just as she had ordered, in perfect health. He had his little bag of groceries that afterwards turned to gold, too.

But somehow or other, eight days afterwards he died.

THINGS THAT HAPPENED LONG AGO

Funny, Funny

Sometimes at night when the corn is ripe in the fields you hear rustling, and louder rustling, and a scream. What is that? It is a *nahual*. It is a nahual stealing.

A nahual can be any shape he chooses. He can be a bird, he can

52

be a bird with a human head. He can be a pig. He can be seen on the road and he looks like a lost pig, but just try to catch him. He runs and runs and it gets dark and then if you keep on running after that funny, funny pig you might fall over a cliff or something. No one can catch a nahual. It is impossible.

He can be a person too. Sometimes he can be a person who lives right down the street and then at night he goes out to steal. Usually you can tell who is a nahual because he always has everything without working for it. He gets it from other people. He is lazy, he steals. A nahual is funny, funny. He is real and yet he isn't real.

Once a man, Pancho was his name, had a wonderful crop of corn and he heard a nahual scream in his field. Naaa . . . oooo . . . wal, just like his name. Out he goes and shoots what he sees. "That will teach him to monkey around with my corn," he said.

The next morning somebody came to the door; one of the neighbors, a man he did not know very well. He did not like him very much. There was something funny, funny about him.

The man said, "My leg is hurt. Would you mind helping to cure it?"

"Oh! So your leg is hurt! Is it a bullet by any chance?"

"Yes, it is a bullet, I guess. Maybe it was you who shot me."

"I did not shoot any man. I only shot at a funny, funny bird that was spoiling my corn."

"But anyhow would you be kind enough to help me now that I'm shot, and give me some breakfast too?"

"No indeed. I will not help a nahual." Saying which, Pancho slammed the door in his face.

The next day Pancho went out to his maguey fields. His magueys were very big. They had longer leaves than any and inside, where the juice collects, there was a lot of it. He got out his sucking-gourd

53

to suck the juice up and get it into a jug to take home and drink. Sweet pulque. He put his gourd into the heart of the plant, then he bent over to suck. Just then, while he was leaning over, a big ram rushed out of the bushes and butted him in the seat of his pants.

Pancho straightened up. "Ouch!" But he didn't see anybody. Nothing. So he leaned over again to suck the pulque, and again the ram rushed out and butted him in the pants. "Ouch! Ouch!" He straightened up and there was nothing.

Funny, funny. Every time he leaned over, something banged him in the pants until he was so bruised and beaten up that he could hardly walk. He had to go home without any pulque to drink.

There was something sitting on his doorstep. It was a bird with a human head. "So!" croaked the bird. "Now you will have to stay in bed and be sick. That will teach you to be kinder to your neighbors, especially when they are hurt." And he opened out his wings and disappeared screaming.

Pancho grew old and rich and his wife grew fat. They had a daughter and she grew up. She fell in love with a boy named Felipe who never did any work. He just liked to lie in the sun and look at the clouds, and his father and mother did all the work. Pancho did not think much of Felipe. He said, "He is as lazy as a nahual." But his daughter wanted to marry Felipe and nobody else. Nobody else would do, nobody. But they said, "No."

Felipe would lie in the sun warming himself and thinking about how he could get married to that girl. His father said, "They are rich, we are poor. Pancho does not want to support you, he wants a

son-in-law who will bring something in, who will work so they can all get richer."

"Work! Who cares about work," said Felipe. "This is love."

So he lay in the sun and thought about the girl, and then he wandered over to her house. There was a big pepper-tree behind the house. Its branches hung low down softly. He climbed into the tree and he began to imitate a nahual. "Naaa . . . oooo . . . wal!"

Pretty soon, he could scream like a real nahual, "Naaa . . . oooo . . . wal!" And he screamed, "If you don't give me your daughter she will go crazy! If you don't give me your daughter she will go crazy!"

He did this every day, singing that same song. Every day for about six months he climbed the tree and told those people that if they did not give him the daughter she would go crazy. Pancho heard him. He did not know. Was Felipe just Felipe or was he really a nahual?

The mother said, "Maybe our daughter will really go crazy. Nahual yes, or nahual no, I do not want my daughter to go crazy. It would be better to let them marry."

So the next morning very early she went to see Felipe. "You can marry our daughter after all," she said.

"Oh," Felipe yawned, "I don't feel like it any more. I begged and begged you for the girl but you would not have me for a son-in-law, and now I have no money and don't feel like getting married."

"Please, please, Felipe, don't be that way. We made a mistake, we are sorry, we do want you for a son-in-law, for my daughter loves you very much."

"But," said Felipe, "who will pay for the wedding and who will take care of us afterwards? I have no money and I do not know how to work. You know how it is, I like to sit in the sun. It's nice."

"We will pay for the wedding and we have enough for everybody, Felipe. You can help if you want to and if you don't want to you don't have to. But we want you for a son-in-law anyway. Our daughter loves you very much."

So Felipe married Pancho's daughter and he turned out to be a good son-in-law after all. But Pancho never found out that he wasn't a real nahual. He was afraid to ask him. Instead he was always very polite to him and Felipe was very polite too, and everybody was polite. So it was a happy family.

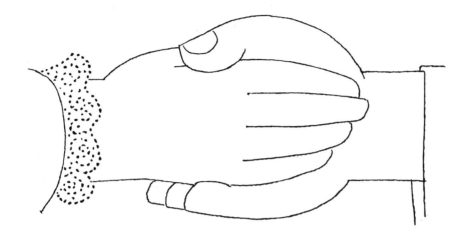

The Princess and Jose

Jose was a good boy and very polite. He liked to learn about other places. So one day he decided to go and see the world.

He was walking along the road when he was arrested. Some soldiers arrested him.

"Why do you arrest me?" said Jose. "I haven't done anything wrong."

"You look like a thief," they said. "Besides, we need prisoners to build the roads."

"I am not a thief," Jose said, "and I don't see why I should work on the roads if I don't want to, especially if I am not paid for it."

"Prisoners aren't paid." That was what the soldiers told him.

Jose stood in the middle of the road and the soldiers were all around him, and he made a speech. They took their guns off their

shoulders and listened. He said, "It is not fair to make people work and not pay for it. I will not do it."

"If you won't work, then you go to jail," said the soldiers. And there he was. In jail. "And if you don't work, you don't eat," they said, so there he was in jail, and hungry.

Now the king of this place had a daughter. She was the princess. She was very beautiful and also very kind. When she heard about Jose she took a basket and packed it full of things to eat, enough for breakfast and dinner and supper. She put in eggs and bread and cake and milk and a whole roast chicken, and pork and beans and chili, of course, and a pineapple and some chocolate candy. She covered it up with a fine white napkin and she got into her golden coach and went to the jail.

There were many prisoners in the jail. They were all going to be shot, one by one. This was because the king had nothing to do. He loved games and riddles but they were all old ones and he was tired of them, so he was peevish. Every time he was peevish he always had somebody shot. That is the way kings are.

Every morning the princess came to the jail with a basket on her arm. It had Jose's food in it. The soldiers let her in. They winked and smiled and said, "The princess must be in love with Jose."

"But it is very sad, they cannot marry because Jose has to be shot," one soldier said.

"Yes, he will be the very first one because he wouldn't work on the roads," said another soldier.

"The next time the king feels like shooting some one, it will be Jose's turn. Too bad."

But the princess said to Jose, "I am looking for a way to save you."

One morning the king woke up feeling very cross. He had noth-

61

ing to do and so he was cross. He decided that Jose would be shot that day. The princess saw how cross he was so she ran to Jose and whispered something, and then she ran out again to where the soldiers were all lined up ready to shoot him.

Everybody was watching. Suddenly the princess spread out a sheet that was nine feet long. Four soldiers had to hold it up. It had something written on it in big red letters. It said, "Father, if he tells you a riddle that you can't guess, will you spare his life?"

"Yes," said the king, "certainly I will. Of course. Naturally." He called to Jose, "If you tell me a riddle that I can't guess, I will spare your life."

There was Jose in the middle of all the soldiers. He looked at the king, then he looked at the princess, then he looked wise. "What is it that goes first on four legs, then on two legs, and then on three legs?" he asked.

The king thought. He thought and thought. He scratched his head until his crown fell off and then he thought some more, but he couldn't guess. "All right," said the king, "your life is saved. But what is the answer?"

"Why, it's very simple. It is yourself. When you were a baby you crawled on all fours. Now you are a man and you walk on two legs. When you grow old, you will have a cane. That will be three. See? First four, then two, then three."

The king was surprised. It was so simple. "Jose must be pretty clever to think of something like that," he said. "It is all right if he wants to marry the princess." So they married. They had a big party and they all ate and sang and danced and Jose opened the jail and let all the other prisoners out.

So they lived in the palace happily but Jose wanted to go and see things and, besides, he wanted to visit his family. He dressed him-

self in his old clothes, the poor man's clothes he was wearing when the soldiers arrested him, and he went home.

In the morning, his father and brothers went out to work in the fields. Jose went with them. At noon his mother brought a basket with his father's dinner in it, and his brothers' wives brought baskets for them.

"Won't you have some dinner?" said Jose's father and brothers, for Jose had no basket.

"Oh, no thank you. I'll have my dinner later," said Jose carelessly.

At that moment they saw a golden coach coming along the road. Then came two other coaches full of soldiers, and some more soldiers on horses. It was the princess in her golden coach, sitting inside with her basket and the soldiers were the escort, because when kings and princesses go any place it is like a parade.

Jose's family was frightened when they saw the soldiers. They wondered if anybody was going to be arrested, but Jose said carelessly, "Oh, that's nothing. It's just my wife bringing my dinner."

The Rabbit Who Wanted to Be a Man

Once there was a happy rabbit. All he did was nibble daisies and clover, and once in a while he stole a carrot from a farmer's field. He was so happy that his tail turned up and his nose wiggled.

But one day the happy rabbit said, "I would like to be a man. Men have everything. They have fields and fields of carrots and turnips and lettuce, and what do I have? All I have is a little hole in the ground."

"The first thing," he said, "is to find a good farm." He did that. "Second, I hire some helpers to do the work." He did that. "Third, I get some seed." He did that. He stole some seed out of a farmer's barn.

Then when the seeds were planted he walked around and said, "Ho! I am just as good as a man."

The turnips grew. They looked wonderful. They looked so good that the rabbit said, "I think I will taste them." Tasting and tasting, he ate them all up. "And now, what will I pay those helpers with?"

When they came, he had nothing. "If you do not pay us we will stop working. We will strike," said the helpers.

"Oh, I will pay you, don't worry. Just wait till I go to the bank," said the rabbit.

He walked along the road and met a cockroach. "Good morning, Mr. Cockroach. How would you like to buy a lot of fine turnips?"

"I will buy them if you let me have them cheap."

"Oh, very cheap. Five dollars. I have just planted them but I need the money to pay my helpers. I will let you know when they are ready."

"All right," said the cockroach, and he gave the rabbit five dollars. They shook hands and the rabbit scampered home to pay his helpers.

Then the tomatoes were almost ready. The rabbit just had to have a little taste, and another little taste, and another, and soon, what do you think? He ate them all up. Now he had to get some money somewhere to pay his helpers. He had no turnips to pay them with, and no tomatoes. So he went along the road and met a rooster.

"Oh, good morning, Mr. Rooster. Would you like to buy a nice crop of tomatoes for five dollars?"

"Five dollars is a lot of money," said the rooster. "Make it four-fifty."

"Five dollars is my price. The tomatoes are almost ripe, you see, and you will make a good profit on it." So the rooster gave him five dollars. "Let me know when they are ready," he said.

The rabbit paid his helpers and then went out to look at his lettuce. By this time he was getting tired of having a farm. He had to watch everything to keep other rabbits from stealing his crops. And then he had to pay his helpers, and he didn't like that. The lettuce looked so crisp and green and nice, he said, "I just must have some to keep the other rabbits from eating it first." And he ate up all the lettuce. This time when he went along the road he met a coyote.

66

"Aha!" he said, "another customer. Being a man is easy, all you do is get a customer." And he sold the lettuce for five dollars to Mr. Coyote. "I will certainly let you know when it is ready," he said.

Finally his last crop came up, it was ripening. It was lovely young corn. What did he do? He thought, "I guess I deserve a little something for all my trouble," and he tasted the corn all up. Then he went out to make arrangements for money again. This time it was a hunter. "How would you like a nice crop of corn very cheap, Mr. Hunter?" he asked.

"Where is it?"

"Oh, it isn't ready yet, but times are so bad I am a little short of money so I have to sell it. I will let you have it for five dollars."

The hunter paid him five dollars and said, "But remember, now, you must let me know when it is ready."

The rabbit paid his helpers and said, "Now there is no more work to do. Good-by." And he spent the summer very happily, saying, "All my worries are over." He slept in the clover and skipped up and down the road wiggling his nose.

But what about the cockroach, the rooster, the coyote, and the hunter? Oh, they were waiting politely for the rabbit to say, "Come and get your crops. They are ready."

One morning the rabbit was skipping along the road and he met the cockroach. "Good morning, Mr. Rabbit," said the cockroach. "You must have a fine crop of turnips by now. When could I come and get them?"

"Oh, good morning, Mr. Cockroach. How are you? How is Mrs. Cockroach? How is little Johnny Cockroach? Nice weather we're having."

"But when can I come for my turnips, Mr. Rabbit?"

"Oh, come tomorrow. I was just coming to let you know." Then he went to see the rooster and the coyote and the hunter and he said to all of them, "Come tomorrow for your crops."

The cockroach arrived first. "Good morning, Mr. Rabbit," he said. "Could I have my turnips now?"

"Why, of course, come right in," said the rabbit. "How are you? How is Mrs. Cockroach and how is little Johnny Cockroach?"

"Just fine, but could I have my turnips please?"

"Oh yes. But wait a minute—doesn't Mr. Rooster happen to be an enemy of yours?"

"I should say so! If he sees me, he eats me," said the Cockroach.

"Well, there he is coming up the road. You'd better hide. Hide under that old kettle."

Up comes the rooster. "Good morning, Mr. Rabbit. I came for my tomatoes."

"Oh yes, come right in, but listen, shsh . . . how would you like a nice bit of cockroach?" the rabbit whispered.

"Oh, I would like that fine, where is it?"

"Right under the kettle." And the rooster went peck, peck, peck, and that was the end of poor Mr. Cockroach.

"Now could I have my tomatoes?" said the rooster.

"Oh yes, but listen, doesn't Mr. Coyote happen to be an enemy of yours? Because there he is coming up the road."

"If he sees me he eats me! Quick, where shall I hide?"

"Oh, in that hole over there by the fire."

Now came the coyote. "Good morning Mr. Rabbit. I came for my lettuce," he said. "I shall take it to market tomorrow and make a good profit on it."

"Oh yes," said the rabbit. "Yes indeed. But would you like a nice meal of rooster first?"

"Why, I would love it. Where is it?"

"Right in that hole by the fire." And the coyote took one snap and another snap and that was the end of poor Mr. Rooster.

"Now could I have my lettuce?" said the coyote.

"Of course, but listen, doesn't Mr. Hunter happen to be an enemy of yours? He is right there at the door."

"Good heavens, yes! Where shall I hide?"

"Shsh . . . come right out and hide behind my spreading prickly pear. Have some of the fruit if you like."

The coyote was so frightened and in such a hurry to eat the fruit of the cactus that he did not notice that it was covered with thorns. He grabbed it and got his paws so full of thorns that he began to cry and he did not hear what the rabbit was saying to the hunter.

"Why, good morning, Mr. Hunter, come right in. I have your corn all ready for you. But first, how would you like to shoot a nice big coyote?"

"Where is he?" asked the hunter.

"Right out there behind my spreading prickly pear."

The hunter took out his gun. Bang! And the little rabbit started to run. Bang! Bang! That was the end of poor Mr. Coyote.

But by that time the rabbit was running as fast as his legs would go. He went a long way and then he sat down to rest and think things over. "I guess it is fine to be a man," said the rabbit. "But it is better to be a rabbit. I had too many bad ideas," he said.

How Flint-Face Lost His Name

He had a very long fine name, but everybody called him Flint-Face. This was because he had such a mean expression on his face. He had a lot of money but he always wanted more. He would lend his money to poor people and charge them twelve per cent interest on it. If he could get more, he would charge still more.

One day he was invited to a party. There were many people there, but none of them as rich as Flint-Face. He was very proud because he was the richest man there. He enjoyed himself very much. It was such a good party that it was very late when it was over. It was very dark. Flint-Face was afraid to go home. He was afraid somebody might do something to him, because he was so rich and so mean.

So he begged his friends to let him stay all night. They said, "Why certainly, you're welcome. You can sleep in the room at the back of the house."

Then Flint-Face went to bed. But he was so rich and so mean that he couldn't sleep. He tossed and he turned and he shook out his pillow but it was no use. Then he thought he might go to sleep if he started counting all the money he had. He counted and counted and counted and counted; ten, twenty, thirty, a hundred, a thousand, five thousand, ten thousand, and soon he was fast asleep.

He had a dream. He dreamed that there was a crowd of beggars at his house. He woke up very much afraid, and ran out without even saying good-by and thank you. He ran and ran and sure enough when he got home there was a big crowd of beggars in front of his house. Some of them had no shoes, and others had no shirts, and none of them had a hair-cut. They were taking his house apart. Taking everything in it.

And they all grabbed him and yelled in his ears, "Flint-Face! Flint-Face! We haven't had any breakfast! We haven't had any dinner! We haven't had any supper!" The more he pushed, the more they yelled.

"Go away from here, you tramps!" said Flint-Face. "Why don't you work for a living?"

But all they said was, "Flint-Face! Flint-Face! We haven't had any breakfast! We haven't had any dinner! We haven't had any supper! Flint-Face! Flint-Face!"

By that time it was morning, and the baker was making his rounds with a load of nice fresh bread. He stopped at old Flint-Face's house and said, "Two cents' worth, as usual?"

"No, how much for the whole load?" said Flint-Face.

"Five dollars," the baker said.

"Five dollars! Oh-me-oh-my, that's way too much! It's robbery! I'll give you four."

"All right," said the baker. "I'll let you have it for four seventy-five, and not one cent less."

So Flint-Face bought the whole load and he started taking the bread out and throwing it at the beggars. They snatched it up and pretty soon they all had enough. So they went away.

Flint-Face ran into his house and the first thing he did was to count his money. It was all there, except for the four dollars and seventy-five cents he had spent on bread. It made him very sad, and very angry. "I'll get even with them," he said to himself. "I won't buy any breakfast and I'll just spend the whole day long collecting money from people."

That is what he did. He went from house to house, making people pay him what they owed him. Even if they told him they were very poor and hungry, it didn't help a bit. He just said, "Well, why don't you go out and work? Look at me, I'm a rich man, but I'm working twice as hard as you are. It's not my fault you're poor." They did not know how to answer him. Besides, they were afraid to.

That night Flint-Face was so tired that he went right to sleep. "Saves me from buying any supper," he said. And he had another dream. He dreamed he was dead. He walked up to the gates of heaven and knocked. Saint Peter came to the door jangling his keys.

"What do you want?" he said.

"I died," said Flint-Face.

"What about it?" said Saint Peter.

"Well, I belong in heaven, don't I?"

"Wait a minute," said Saint Peter, "I'll go ask the Lord."

Then the Lord came to the door and said, "What do you want?"

"I died," said Flint-Face.

"What about it?" said the Lord.

"Nothing, only naturally since I am a rich man I have the best of everything. So it's clear I belong in heaven."

"Is that so?" said the Lord. "Why do you want to come to heaven? You never thought about it before."

"Well, of course I never thought about it because I was too busy. But I come of a fine family and I guess that entitles me to mingle in the best circles."

"Yes, but you're a wicked man," said the Lord.

"Indeed I am not! I was never in jail in my life!"

"But you lend money and charge twelve per cent interest," said the Lord.

"That's perfectly legal, isn't it? I never did a dishonest thing in my life."

"Yes, it is legal all right," said the Lord, "but it isn't right. You have to be a good man if you want to go to heaven."

73

"I bought four dollars and seventy-five cents' worth of bread for some beggars this very morning!"

"Yes, but you threw it at them. And besides, that's not enough."

"Last Christmas I had the church painted. It cost me a lot of money too."

"Wait a minute, I'll look in the books," said the Lord. He brought out a big black book and turned to page nine hundred and twenty-seven. "Yes, here it is. But I'm afraid that isn't enough either."

"But why not? I'm getting awfully tired of waiting out here in the cold. Nobody ever treated me like this before. Besides, Christmas before last I gave some money to the orphanage."

"Yes, that's here in the books too. But you never did anything for anybody because you really wanted to. You can't get into heaven with money. It's against the rules. You never loved anything but your money. It wasn't your money anyway."

"I'd like to know why it wasn't!" said Flint-Face.

"Go home and figure it out. Nobody asked you to come here," and the Lord slammed the gates of heaven right in his face.

Then Flint-Face woke up. It was morning. The first thing he did was to run to his money-box to see if all the money he had collected the day before was still there. Every bit of it was gone! All the money he had accumulated for so many years was gone too! And he hadn't a friend in the world, because he had always been so mean.

There was nothing to do but beg. So Flint-Face became a beggar, and he was very much ashamed of himself for everything he had done. But nobody ever called him Flint-Face again.

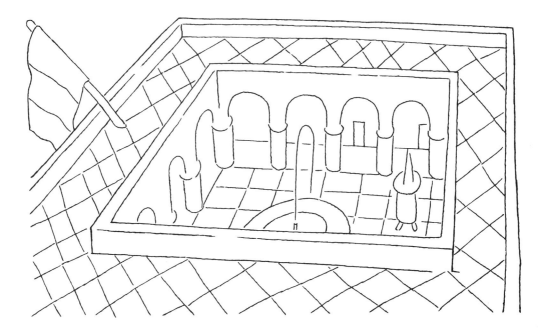

One Roll of Bread

This was a poor man who had many children. Sometimes he did not earn much money and they did not have enough to eat, not enough to go around. So then he would beg.

In that place there was a prince who was very rich but he was not like most of the rich people, for he was kind. One day this poor man who had so many children just could not find a job, no work, no money, no food, no anything. He was on the street begging and the prince saw him. The prince came to where he was but the poor man was ashamed, he was so dirty and ragged. So he walked away quickly. The prince followed him, talking in a gentle way but the poor man went faster and faster and the prince went faster too, and soon they were almost running. Finally the poor man was out of breath. He stopped and allowed the prince to talk to him. The prince said, "Please come to my palace with me, poor man."

They went up the marble steps of the palace and there, inside, the prince gave him clothes for all the children, and groceries, and some money to help him meet his many needs. The prince said, "Please promise me something. Come to the palace every two weeks on Monday to get food."

So two weeks later he came to the palace, but the prince was not there. He said, "I believe there was a message for me?"

"Yes," said the housekeeper. "Here is your message." And she gave him one roll of bread.

One roll. What can you do with one roll of bread for a big family with many children? The poor man didn't say anything, he just thanked the housekeeper politely and went away feeling sad. He sold the bread to a bakery and with the money he bought some corn. "It goes further," he said. "And it is more filling."

After that he came to the palace every two weeks on Monday, and every two weeks on Monday the housekeeper said, "Here is your message," and gave him one roll of bread.

The poor man could not understand it. He thought, "They have strange ways," but he thanked them politely and sold the bread and bought corn instead.

One day when he came to the palace the prince was there. He said, "Listen, my son, what do you do with all the bread we give you here?"

"Your Majesty, what does anybody do with bread?" said the poor man. He could not say anything else, such as for instance, "One roll is not enough, so I sell it and buy corn." It wouldn't be polite.

It was all very strange because the prince said, "Then why are you still so poor and miserable?"

"I guess it is all a matter of luck, Your Majesty," said the poor man. But the prince was not satisfied with that answer.

"If you ate the bread I am sure you would not be so poor any more," said the prince.

It sounded silly to the man so he didn't answer. What could he say?

"Now listen," said the prince. "Today I am going to give you another roll of bread, but you must absolutely eat it because if you don't, I will never help you again."

This poor man left the palace very much bewildered. He thought, "These rich people have funny ideas. One roll of bread!"

He was going to sell it again and he stopped in front of the bakery, but he noticed there was nothing in the window any more. There was only a sign that said, *Gone Out of Business. We Have Enough Money So We Do Not Have to Work Any More.*

He went home sadly, thinking how nice it would be to have enough money like the baker. "He has been lucky," he said.

He got home and said to his wife and children, "I apologize, but all I have for you is just one roll of bread. The prince said we absolutely must eat it. That if we did not, he would never help us again."

They sat down at their long long table, there were so many of them, and the poor man began to break the one roll of bread into little pieces. When he did that, a gold piece, a fifty dollar gold piece, fell out of the roll.

"Oh, that explains everything! There must have been money in every roll of bread I sold the baker! Now he is rich and here we are just where we were before. How foolish I have been. I have been selling bread and giving away happiness."

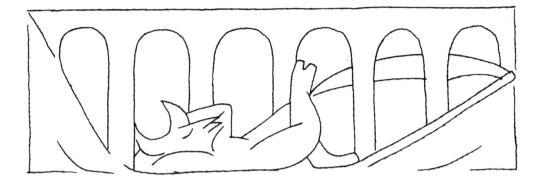

The Devil and the Railroad

This happened many years ago when people were just beginning to build railroads. They were building this one through the mountains. Everything went along very well until they came to a deep canyon. They had to make a bridge over it. It was hard to do. They had to put a lot of men to work on it.

But something very queer was going on. They couldn't seem to get the bridge finished. One day the superintendent came around. He said, "What is the matter here? You've been working and working and still the bridge isn't finished. I suppose you sleep all day instead of working."

"No sir," they told him. "We don't sleep a bit. We work very hard. Something seems to be wrong with that bridge. Every day we build it up and the next morning it's all torn down. We don't know what can be the matter. Of course we are not engineers, we're just ordinary laborers. Maybe you could explain it."

"You say the bridge is all built every night and the next morning it is torn down again?"

"Yes, sir."

"That's funny. Very funny indeed," said the superintendent. He put his head in his hands and started to think. He thought and thought, and then he took out a pencil and a piece of paper and made a lot of calculations. Finally he decided he would hide near the bridge and see what happened.

So that night the superintendent crawled into a cave over the bridge and sat very still. Pretty soon he looked at his watch and it was eleven o'clock. Just then he heard an automobile. "That's queer," he said to himself. "How can an automobile come here, especially as there is no road?" He held his breath and waited.

The automobile drove up and stopped right under the bridge. It was a big shiny car. The superintendent couldn't tell exactly what kind it was because it was so dark. He saw a man step out of the car. He was a big man, all dressed up. He must have been about seven feet high and he was wide too. He had a diamond in his shirt. The superintendent could see it sparkle. He had a tall hat on, which made him look still bigger.

The superintendent thought perhaps he was a banker coming to see how the railroad was getting along. But it was queer for a banker to come way out here, and how could he drive an automobile when there was no road? "Well, he's here for no good, I'm sure of that. I'll just wait and see," thought the superintendent.

Then the big man went over to the bridge and began doing something in the dark. The superintendent could not see but he heard something crack. Then one of the bridge-pillars crashed down and the whole bridge began to crumble.

The superintendent jumped out. "Hey, you, what are you doing to my bridge? I will have you arrested for destroying property."

But the big man just sneered at him and walked away. So the superintendent hit him. He hit him so hard it knocked his hat off, and then he saw something funny. The big man had two little horns sticking out of his bald head! No hair at all, only the horns!

"Aha! I thought there was something funny about you!" he said. "What do you mean by breaking up our bridge like that? Don't you know it costs a lot of money?"

"I don't like your old bridge," said the fat man. "This is my favorite place and it is where I have my summer home. I won't have your old railroad making a lot of noise and dirt here."

"But don't you realize it's progress?" said the superintendent. "Do you want to stand in our way like that? You are mean."

"I guess you don't know who I am, do you? I am Satan. Some people call me the devil. I will let you build your bridge . . . if you pay me my price."

"How much do you want? We can't afford much because it's hard times and you've made us lose a lot of money on this bridge."

"I don't want any money. I'm the richest man there is, anyway. But if you will give me two hundred human heads, I will let you build your bridge."

"Two hundred is way too much," said the superintendent. "And I can't deal with you anyhow. I have to call a meeting. Tomorrow night I'll come back here and tell you what they said."

The next night when the superintendent met the devil, he took out his pencil and notebook and made a lot of calculations. "See here," he said, "we can't afford two hundred heads. We'll give you a hundred and fifty, on condition that you build the bridge yourself."

"That's fine," said the devil. "Let's make a contract."

So the devil and the superintendent drew up a contract, and this is what the contract said:

Whereas, I am the devil and don't like railroads; Whereas, you are the superintendent and are building one; I, the devil, will build

81

it for you, myself and without help and without cost to anybody else, on the condition that you, the superintendent, will pay me one hundred and fifty souls on the night that the bridge is finished. This will be midnight tomorrow and I, the devil, agree to have the bridge finished by the time the first cock crows, and if this is not done this contract shall be null and void and I will not receive payment for same.

"But that can't happen," said the devil laughing. "I have made a good bargain here."

"Wait and see, wait and see," said the superintendent, and they shook hands and went away.

On the night the bridge was supposed to be finished, the superintendent came to see what had happened. He was a very clever man. He looked at the bridge and took out his pencil and notebook and made a lot of calculations. Then he opened a bag he had and took out a rooster and an alarm clock. He hid himself on the bridge.

Pretty soon he took out his watch. It was ten-thirty. He set the alarm clock at a quarter to twelve and he put it down next to the rooster. The devil was so busy trying to finish the bridge that he didn't notice what was going on.

At a quarter to twelve the bridge was almost finished. But suddenly the alarm clock went, "Ding, ding, di-i-i-i-ng!"

And when the rooster heard it he thought it was morning, so he crowed and flapped his wings. "Cockadoodle-doooooo! Cockadoodledoooo!"

The devil looked up very much surprised. The superintendent was sitting there laughing and laughing. "Ha, ha, ha! It's midnight and the bridge isn't finished! Ha, ha, ha!"

"What do you mean, midnight! It's only ten minutes to twelve!"

"Oh, no it isn't. It's twelve o'clock. Look at the alarm clock," said

82

the superintendent. "And besides, can a rooster make a mistake?"

"Well, I guess you win," said the devil. "I guess my watch must be slow. I would have finished in another ten minutes." And he went away suspicious and angry. But the bridge was built.

The only trouble was that the first time a train ran over it, the devil was so mad that he wrecked it. Three hundred people were killed. Which just shows that the devil gets his share in the end.

The Boy Who Beat the Devil

His name was Julian. When he was about eight years old he wanted to know everything. He loved to read and he wanted to learn so many things that he began everything, but he didn't finish anything.

He grew. He still wanted to know everything, he began everything. First he decided to be a lawyer. He studied law for one year but then he stopped. He said, "Why be a lawyer? I don't think I could get so far as to be a judge, and if I did, who wants to be a judge? I wouldn't. I would be too sorry for the people I had to send to jail. I think I will be a doctor."

So he studied to be a doctor. He did that for two years. Then he said, "How dreadful to be around sick people all the time. No, this wasn't intended for the son of my mother. Better to be a druggist. No, on second thought, no. I couldn't stand the smell of all the drugs. Therefore I shall be a veterinarian. But examined closely, that idea does not please me either. If I do not want to be around sick people all the time, why should I be around sick animals?"

He thought of many professions but there was something the matter with all of them. He read many books. "I shall do something pleasant," he said. "I shall be a musician." So he took all his money and he bought musical instruments. He bought two clarinets, a horn, three violins, two drums, and some tympani. Then he went and said to the municipal president, "Sir, I have an orchestra. Moreover, I have composed a piece in your honor. It is a piece that consists of forty-two different sounds."

The musicians were invited to go to the municipal palace and play their splendid music. They took their seats. Julian began to conduct, they began to play. It was very new. The municipal president did not like it at all. The music annoyed him so much that he kicked Julian, the orchestra director. He kicked him so hard that he dropped his baton. Then he kicked him out of the palace. "By this road," said Julian, "I will get no place."

Now he was a poor man. He went to the woods and there he met some shepherds with their flocks. He begged them to hire him as an assistant and general servant, so they did. He went out with the sheep next morning, to a pasture near a river. When the hour of rest after lunch came, he lay down in the shade of a tree and went to sleep.

He had barely closed his eyes when he heard a strange noise, it sounded like an earthquake. It was coming from under the ground. He woke up and came to himself and looked at the sheep. "Those sheep are acting very strangely," he said. "Very odd." As he looked, he saw them slowly turning into devils. The pasture was so full of devils it looked like a ballroom in hell. Then the tree under which Julian was standing began to act strange, too. It turned into Satan himself. Some people call him Lucifer, the chief of the devils. "Oh my, what peculiar sheep I have been looking after!" Julian said. "I didn't know these gentry ever wore wool!"

"Gentlemen! Gentlemen devils, little devils, devilets, and deviltons," said Lucifer, shaking a rattle that hung on one of his horns, "I have called you together today to hear from you. I want to have your reports. What has each one thought up to tease and displease these humans?" Then each demon stood up and talked, telling the mischief he had done. But one of the little devils had nothing to report. He had been playing all the time instead of attending to devil-business. So now he took a bundle of fire-crackers and tied them to Lucifer's tail. Then he set fire to them.

The effect was immediate. Lucifer rose off the earth and ripped into the sky, carried by the fire-crackers. Showers of flaming gunpowder dropped all over him, making him very uncomfortable and burning his eyes. "Brutes, scoundrels," yelled Lucifer from on high. "What a way of making me leave the earth! . . . Am I going to wipe out the imbecile who did this!"

The fire-crackers now exploded all at once, a hundred times in a hundred directions and the devil, with his wings torn and his head dizzy with the noise, banged down with tremendous force on the ground. He was stunned by the blow. The other devils, devilets, and deviltons ran away frightened.

Julian saw his opportunity. He came forward quickly and grabbed the devil by the tail and, dragging him over the ground, broke his horns and his fangs against the rocks. It made quite a loud noise and the shepherds came running to see what was happening. When they saw that the devil was caught, they at once removed their belts and with them gave a great beating to the enemy of mankind.

"Let me go home," cried the devil, "and I will make you rich!"

"Harder, boys!" said Julian.

"Let me go or I will turn you into dust and ashes!"

"Still harder, friends!" Julian shouted.

To escape all this the devil turned himself into a pond, and there were all the sheep swimming around in it. But Julian knew a little about white magic because he had read so many books, and he turned the shepherds into little fish that bit the sheep and the water.

The pond disappeared. Instead appeared a great tree, but Julian knew a little of everything so he knew about that too, and he turned the shepherds into birds that picked at the fruit of the tree. This way and that way they molested the devil, just as the devil molests men.

Lucifer didn't like it. Suddenly the ground opened up with a great roar, and fire came out of it. There was the devil standing on the edge. People came running out of their houses to see what the noise was and the shepherds' wives got there first. They saw the devil standing on the edge of the fiery pit and he was pointing into it.

"Now let's see you follow me down there!" he snarled. And then he jumped in, followed by all the devils, devilets, and deviltons. Then the hole closed up and disappeared and the pasture was green once more.

88

The shepherds shook hands, saying, "Let us congratulate ourselves that we have such a wise man as Julian with us."

But Julian said suddenly, "Where is our flock of sheep?"

"You ought to know," they answered. "We certainly don't. And you'd better find it because it was a very valuable flock and we won't stand for the loss of it. No indeed."

Julian took out a whistle and blew it in a certain way he knew how. At once the lost sheep began returning from all sides. So the shepherds were satisfied.

After that Julian was a famous man. He was a hermit, he lived in the woods and people came to ask his advice about things. Sometimes the devil would interfere and try to tempt him. Then Julian would say, "Do you remember that beating I gave you?" And the devil would make a sour face and go up in smoke.

The Bow, the Deer, & the Talking Bird

A rich Aztec merchant was dying and he called his three sons and said, "My sons, my time upon this earth is ended. I have tried to be a loyal friend, an honest merchant, and a brave warrior. I have educated you as well as I was able and I hope that if I have any enemies it is more because of their envy than for any wickedness of mine. Besides my advice and example, I wish to leave you three things. If managed properly, they will be better than the greatest riches. These three things are a bow that always sends the arrow

90

true to its aim, a deer that will take his master anywhere he wants to go, and a bird that speaks of what it sees." He died.

The eldest son said, "As I am the eldest, I should have first choice of the inheritance. I choose the bow." For he thought to himself, "With a bow like that I can kill the rarest birds and become a rich trader in fine feathers and plumes."

The second son said, "Between a gabby-bird and a deer that will take me anywhere I want to go, I choose the deer."

So the youngest son took what was left; the bird. He thought, "I will take care of it lovingly, there may not be much use in a bird like that but it belonged to my dear father." Then they all went off to seek their fortunes.

Many years later the two oldest brothers heard that the youngest one was now a great and famous man. He was the Prime Minister to the king. His advice and warnings and opinions were listened to, for they were always wise and true. The two brothers became very jealous when they heard this, and they plotted to kill him, steal the bird that they had so thoughtlessly refused, and take their brother's place. They well knew that it was the wonderful bird that had made him Prime Minister.

They did not notice that while they were talking, the very same bird was sitting on a branch above their heads. He heard them, and flew to tell the youngest son. Tears came to his eyes. "Alas," he said, "I am not afraid of my brothers. I can take care of myself, but my poor father's ghost must be distressed to learn that his sons are un-worthy of him. I do not think they are really bad at heart. Let us see what can be done."

The next day the two brothers arrived at the king's court. They pretended to be overcome with surprise and joy at their youngest brother's luck in being such an important man. He received them with tears in his eyes and gave them the best rooms in the palace, and introduced them to the king, too. The brothers went to sleep early, for the eldest was tired from walking so far and the second brother had a sore throat from the dust that his deer had made as it ran swiftly along the roads.

The youngest son sat down as he did every evening to listen to his little bird. The bird perched on his shoulder and said softly, "The king of the country next to ours has decided to make war on us and conquer us. He wants to take us by surprise. His army will march against us and attack early tomorrow morning. They will take the road that lies below the steep cliff at the mouth of the river." When the bird finished whispering this information into his master's ear, he flew away. But the young man went to the king at once and told him what was going to happen.

"Oh dear, oh dear," said the king. "Our best captains are off on a picnic and the soldiers are having a holiday. What shall we do?"

"Most worthy Sire," said the youngest brother, "if Your Majesty promises to make nobles of my brothers and myself, we three will save you no matter how strong the enemy turns out to be."

"I promise," said the king, but he didn't have much hope. He didn't see how three young men, no matter how brave, could stop all the armies of his powerful neighbor.

The youngest one hurried to his brothers and woke them. "My brothers," he said, "our father was such a brave man that still today, people say when they hear our name, oh, yes, they are the sons of that warrior who never knew what it was to be afraid. Don't you think we are obliged to uphold his reputation and for the honor of our name, go out and defend our native land?" Then he explained what was going to happen. And he made plans.

92

"Your little deer," said he to the middle brother, "will take us to the cliff quickly, in plenty of time, because what army can travel as fast and far as a deer? Then when we get there my bird will tell us exactly where the enemy is hiding. And you with your bow," he said to the eldest brother, "can do the shooting."

The three brothers climbed on the deer's back, and the bird perched on the youngest one's shoulder. The middle brother said, "Quickly, quickly, little deer," and in less than a minute, even less than a second, they were at the cliff. They hid in some bushes and the bird went off on a scouting trip, to see what he could see. He came back quickly and told them where the enemy was hidden, and exactly where the king of the attacking soldiers was.

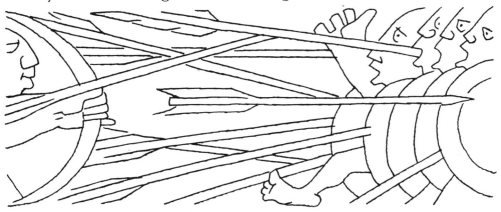

The eldest brother fitted an arrow to his bow, aimed where the little bird told him, and shot. The arrow travelled far away where the wicked king was hiding, whang! through his heart. The army was frightened and bewildered. The soldiers said, "This is very strange, let us go home." But one captain, bolder than the others, jumped up and shouted, "Forward, my brave boys, let us avenge the death of our great and noble king!" The eldest brother fitted another arrow to his bow, aimed at the captain, and the arrow travelled far and fast, whang! And the captain fell dead.

The soldiers began to run back to their own country as fast as they could. By the time the sun rose they were all gone, running, some on galloping horses, some on foot. The three brothers put the dead king and the dead captain on the deer's back, and they all went home to breakfast.

The people came out to meet them, singing and dancing and cheering. The king made nobles of the three brothers and gave them rich presents, lands, houses, horses, wonderful things. They lived happily after that because they had found out something important: that together they could do more than separately, and that there is nothing better than a good brother. Ever since then, when people know a secret, they say, "Oh, a little bird told me."

TALES OF MAGIC, BLACK AND WHITE

The Dead Man Who Was Alive

This happened many years ago, after a war. Many people die in a war and there is no time to bury them all, because everybody is busy killing more. So the wind carries the decay and this always does great harm.

A very terrible disease started going around. The name of it was Yellow Cholera. It went everywhere and day by day people would get sick and die. Everybody was so afraid of this Yellow Cholera that they buried the people who died of it right away, the minute they died. So many queer things happened.

Well, there was a nice man named Pedro who helped to bury the people. Sometimes he just could not believe they were dead at all. So he made them very comfortable in their graves and always put some water and a loaf of bread in, just in case they got hungry or anything.

Then Pedro got sick too, and he died. They took him and buried him right away. There was no time to make him a nice coffin but they put a new mat down in the grave and some water and some bread, and they laid him down and covered him up quick.

After a while the Yellow Cholera stopped and the cemetery was

96

very still. But some people went there to visit the graves, and one day they stopped where this nice man named Pedro was buried. There was a little boy with them, and he saw a bug on top of the grave. He stamped on it to kill it. All of a sudden they heard Pedro say, "Would you please do me the favor of not stepping so hard on my grave? Because you are shaking a lot of dirt down on me, and it's getting into my eyes."

"But aren't you dead, Pedro?" the people said.

"Well, I am and I am not. It's very funny about that."

Naturally the first thing they did was to go and tell the priest, because he knew more about such things than they did, and here was something that had never happened before. Usually dead people don't talk. The priest came and tapped gently on the grave, and said, "Hello, there, Pedro!"

"Hello!" said Pedro.

"Would you like to come out?" said the priest.

"Well, I wouldn't mind getting a breath of fresh air," Pedro answered.

They dug him up, but not too hard, because Pedro was saying, "Be careful, now, you're getting dirt all over me." Finally they got down to where he was. He was sitting on his mat with his arms on his knees, and he looked fine except that he was a little pale. He climbed out and shook hands with everybody.

"Well," said the priest, "do you mean to say that you're dead?"

"I guess I am," said Pedro.

"Did it hurt to die?" asked the little boy.

"No, why should it?" said Pedro.

"But how did you live down there all the time?" the boy wanted to know.

"Why, I had some water, and some bread, and of course I wasn't

JC

doing any work or anything, so I wasn't very hungry and it lasted a long time."

"And what did you do down there all the time?" asked the priest.

"Why, I just thought," Pedro said. "I always liked to sit down in a quiet place and think about things. So that is what I did."

"I guess you had better come home with me," the priest said.

"No, I suppose I'll have to find myself a job," Pedro answered.

"I'll give you a job. You can ring the bells in the church," the priest told him. "How would you like that?"

"That would be fine," said Pedro. So he went to live with the priest and he enjoyed ringing the church bells every morning and every evening. But many people said it wasn't true that Pedro had died. They said it was impossible. They explained it by saying that Pedro was crazy.

The Cow That Cried

This is the story of a cow that cried. A man named Florencio heard it.

Florencio was very poor. But he managed to get along because every morning he went to the stockyards and bought the insides of the cattle that were killed for the butchers. They were very cheap. His wife cleaned them and boiled them and these two poor people sold them. They ate some of them. Florencio liked them very much.

Now Florencio had a neighbor, a woman named Margarita. One

day she came to his house to borrow some salt. She saw Florencio eating the insides of the cattle. And she said, "Florencio, do you buy those down at the stockyards that are near the river?"

"Yes," said Florencio, "I buy them because they are so cheap."

"Do you mean at the stockyards that are near the cemetery?"

"Yes," said Florencio. "What about it?"

"They come out of animals that aren't really animals. They're ghosts," said Margarita.

"What nonsense women talk! How do you know they aren't really animals? Can you prove it?"

"No, I can't prove it, but I know it is so anyhow," said Margarita. "The priest does it. He is a bad priest."

"It's wicked to talk that way about priests," Florencio told her. "Don't ever mention it to me again."

So Margarita went away. But not long afterwards, she died.

"Serves her right," said Florencio, "for talking nonsense." And he went right on buying the insides as usual, and eating them.

One day he was waiting at the gate of the stockyards. They hadn't killed the cattle yet. So he sat down and while he was sitting there he saw the cattle come in. He heard a strange thing. He heard one bull say to another, "Is this your first time at the stockyard?"

"No, it is my third time. How many times have you been here?"

"This is my first time," said the bull. "Does it hurt very much when they cut off one's head?"

"No, not so much. It just bleeds."

"And when they cut off the neck?"

"Why no, it doesn't hurt a bit. Just hold stiff, brace yourself, and you won't feel a thing."

Florencio listened and thought it all very strange. Pretty soon he saw a cow come in. There were big tears in her eyes, they were

rolling down her nose. Florencio had never seen a cow cry before so he went right up to her, and said, "What's the matter, cow? Are you sick or anything?"

"No, I'm not sick," said the cow. "I'm just crying because I died. I was all alone in the world and there's nobody to cry for me, so I have to do the crying myself. Moo-hoo!"

"But you're not dead at all," said Florencio.

"Oh, yes I am. Don't you know who I am?"

"Why no, who are you?"

"I am Margarita, you know, who died. I died because I told you about the wicked priest making people into cattle."

"But how can he do that?" asked Florencio.

"It's very simple. He goes to the cemetery at midnight, together with the sacristan. He begins to say prayers backward and do all sorts of strange things. This is Black Magic. Pretty soon the graves open and the dead people come out rubbing their eyes and holding their mats around them. And he and the sacristan go around with some white powder in their hands and they say to the people, who aren't really people but just ghosts, 'Welick! Welick!' This means 'Sweet! Sweet!' So all the people take some and gradually they turn into cattle. Then the priest and the sacristan drive them into the stockyards and slaughter them and sell the beef."

"What nonsense women talk!" said Florencio. "I don't believe a word of it."

He waited until the cattle were butchered and took the insides just as usual. And his wife cleaned them and put them on the fire. Pretty soon she came out with a spoonful and said, "Well, would you like to taste them?"

"I don't think I'd care for any," said Florencio.

"What's the matter? Did you hear anything?" said his wife.

"Well, I did and I didn't," said Florencio. "Besides, it's just women's nonsense, that's all." Then he told her all about the conversation between the bulls, and the cow that cried.

"Aha!" said his wife. "Didn't she tell you?"

"I don't believe it anyway. There must be some other explanation. I'm going right to the priest and ask him if it's true."

"Oh, no, don't do that," cried his wife. "Please don't."

"I guess I know what I'm doing," Florencio said. And he went down to the church.

But his wife was so worried that she went too, and took both their little children along. Florencio made them wait at the door. He went in by himself.

The priest said, "Good morning, Florencio, what can I do for you?"

"Good morning, sir," Florencio answered, "I just came to ask you if it is true that you turn people into cattle. Not people I mean, just ghosts."

"Of course it isn't true," said the priest. "It's impossible. Who told you about it?"

"Margarita told me."

"Oh, she did, did she? And did you tell anybody?"

"No, just my wife."

"Hmm," said the priest. "Hmm, hmmm, hmmm, hmmmm!"

And that was the last of Florencio. His wife and children waited and waited at the door of the church, but they didn't see him. All they saw was a great big bull with heavy hoofs and a long dirty tail. It walked right out of the church, which they thought was a little strange.

After Florencio's wife had waited a long, long time she went inside the church to look for her husband. He wasn't there. Only the priest was there. "Good morning, what can I do for you, Mrs. Florencio?"

"Nothing, sir, I just came to look for my husband, Florencio. He came in. Have you seen him?"

"Of course not. Nobody has been here at all."

So Mrs. Florencio took her two children and went home sadly. She thought to herself, how stubborn men are. And Florencio did not come home again. Only, something else that was very peculiar happened. It is the story of how Mrs. Florencio became a bull-fighter.

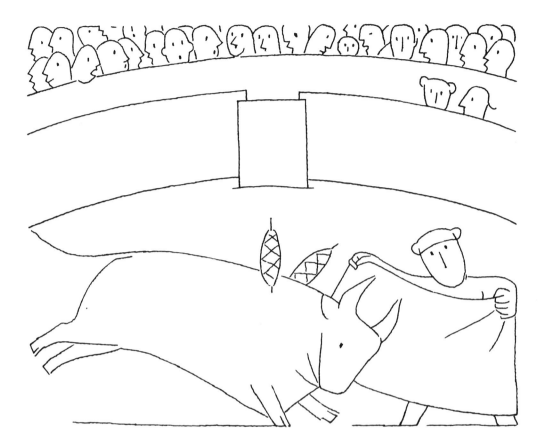

The Poor Widow Bullfighter

When Florencio disappeared, everybody was sure he was dead. That made his wife a widow. And as her own name was Mariposa, everybody called her the Widow Mariposa.

The worst of it was that she did not know how to support her family. All she could think of was to help her neighbors grind corn. Of course this gave her something to eat, and something to take home for her children too. But she had the oldest, raggedest clothes.

And her children, too, could be seen going down the street in rags.

One day she was standing sadly in a cornfield when suddenly she heard a swishing noise. And right in front of her appeared a young man whom she had never seen before. He looked like an ordinary person, but she had never seen an ordinary person appear out of thin air.

"Don't be sad," said this person. "You used to weave pretty sashes and ribbons and girdles. Why don't you make some now, and sell them?"

"I have no wool," said Mariposa.

"I will give you all the wool you want," said the young man. He reached up and reached down, and suddenly Mariposa's hands were full of yarn. There were all the colors of the rainbow.

"Oh, thank you! You must be Tepozton," cried Mariposa.

"Yes. Take good care of your children, and don't cry any more." Then Tepozton suddenly wasn't there any more. On the spot where he had been standing, Mariposa saw a lovely green flower beginning to bloom.

So Mariposa made sashes and hair-bands and sold them. She and her children had plenty to eat, and pretty clothes. But one day she got sick. She could not weave any more. Her children were hungry again. Finally Mariposa went to a neighbor's house to grind corn. But she took it home with her so that nobody should see how sick she was.

She worked and worked, and she got so tired that she just sat down and cried. "Oh, if my husband were alive, I wouldn't be suffering like this," she cried. The minute she said that, a very strange thing happened. A big bull walked right into the house.

The bull bellowed, "Quick, quick, close the door." So Mariposa closed the door.

Then the bull said, "Take this rope off my neck and hide it quickly. And if anybody comes here looking for me, say I'm not here." And suddenly he wasn't a bull any more. He was Florencio!

Florencio told Mariposa that he had just run away from the bull ring. They would surely come looking for him. Now that he was a man it was easy to hide him. She rolled him up in a big mat and laid him down in the corner.

Soon a big crowd of people came to the door. "Have you seen a bull around here?"

"Why, no," Mariposa answered. "I haven't noticed a bull or anything like that." They didn't believe her. They saw the print of the bull's hooves inside the door. But they couldn't see a bull any place. They looked in every corner, and behind the door, and under the bed, and one even started to look in the mat that Florencio was rolled up in. But the widow said, "How silly! Who ever heard of a bull being rolled up in a mat?" So they went away.

Florencio came out and kissed his wife and took his children in his arms. He played with them. He stayed a long time. Then the bells in the church began to ring and Florencio started turning back into a bull again. Mariposa cried and cried.

"Now listen," said the bull. "I can't stay with you because I am under a spell. It is Black Magic. But at least I can help you. To-morrow there is going to be a big bullfight, and I am going to be the third bull in the ring. I will be black all over with white spots on my chest and a white tassel on my tail. And I am going to be very fierce. I won't let anybody get near me. This will tire them out. Then you say that you are going to be a bullfighter. You will show them how. Don't do it too easily. Take the red cape and wave it and dance around and show them it is hard to do. You will win in the end, and there is a prize of a thousand pesos for the best bullfighter. You can live happily ever after."

"But I am sick," said the Widow Mariposa.

"Don't be silly. Now remember, the third bull, black with white spots on the chest and a white tassel at the end of his tail. Goodby." And he galloped away.

The next day, the Widow Mariposa felt better. She decided to go to the bullfight after all. So she put on her best blue shawl and red petticoat and found herself a seat down in front nearest the bull ring. The first bull that came out was big and black and had white spots on his back. He had a sad and tired look on his face, but he bellowed loudly and tried to look very ferocious. A man went into the ring and threw a lasso around his feet and pulled him down. "That's not the one," said Mariposa.

Now came a bigger, blacker bull with white spots on his head. He pawed the ground and shook his horns and stuck out his tongue and bellowed so loudly that Mariposa put her fingers in her ears and wondered, "Could that be my husband Florencio?"

Everybody was afraid of this bull. It took three men to get him down and they were very proud of themselves. "I guess that's the wrong one too," said Mariposa.

The next bull didn't wait for them to open the gate but crashed right through it so that the splinters flew in all directions. He came in so fast that Mariposa couldn't tell what color he was, and he charged right across the ring and stopped in front of where she was and roared so fiercely that all the other people moved back. But she looked at him and saw the white spots on his chest and a white tassel at the end of his tail and she thought she saw a funny look in his eyes. The men started to fight this bull. The first one who came out

109

danced up to the bull and said, "Huh, huh," but the bull picked him up with the tips of his horns and threw him into Mariposa's lap.

"That is more like Florencio," she said.

Then another man came out and the bull frightened him so much that he ran away and has never been heard of since.

Something happened with every one, until at last the president of the bullfight said, "I guess we'll have to take this bull out. He's too fierce."

"This must be the one," said the Widow Mariposa. So she went up to one of the bullfighters and said, "Please, sir, could I borrow your red cape?"

"What do you want my red cape for?"

"I'm going to play that bull," said the Widow Mariposa.

"How ridiculous! Who ever heard of a woman bullfighter? If you want to make a laughing-stock out of yourself . . . why don't you use your red petticoat?"

The Widow Mariposa then went to the president of the bullfight and said, "Please, sir, would you mind letting me try that bull?"

"But what will you use for a cape?" said the president.

"Why, my red flannel petticoat," said the poor widow bullfighter.

"Ha, ha, ha!" laughed the president. "All right, but everybody will laugh at you. And understand, we are not responsible if the bull kills you, neither can we take charge of the poor innocent children that you leave."

"All right, if the bull kills me I'll be dead," said Mariposa calmly. But she knew that nothing could happen to her because the bull was really Florencio.

So she jumped into the ring and waved her red flannel petticoat.

111

"Ha, ha, ha! Look at the Widow Mariposa! She thinks she's a bull-fighter!" everybody cried.

But after a while they stopped laughing. They saw how Mariposa danced around the ring, and the bull roared and ran at her but she dodged him so neatly that nothing happened to her. Finally she took two little spears that were trimmed with colored tissue paper and she waved them at the bull. "Huh, huh, huh!" she grunted, just like a real bullfighter. And the bull bellowed and roared and ran at her, and she stood on her toes and jumped. She landed on his back and rode him all around the ring. The band played and played and everybody clapped.

So Mariposa won the prize for being the best bullfighter. She never had to worry about money again. Everybody called her the Poor Widow Bullfighter, but she really wasn't poor any more.

But a long time afterward, something happened that broke the spell that the wicked priest had put on Florencio. It happened because of a little boy named Chucho.

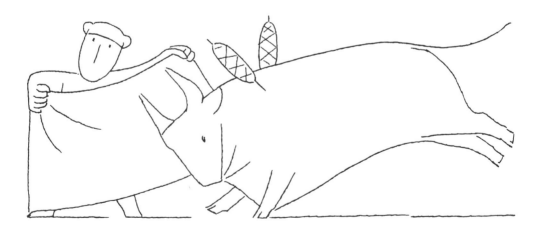

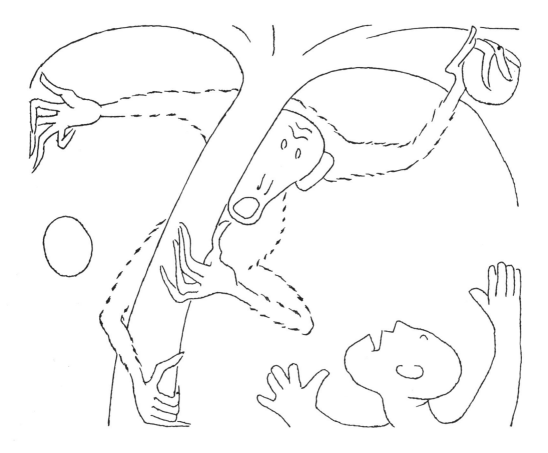

Chucho, Who's Afraid?

Chucho lived in a cave with his father and mother. They made
themselves comfortable there. Chucho's mother cooked over a fire
in the middle of the cave and they slept on mats just like a house in
Milpa Alta. Outside the cave Chucho's father planted a corn-patch,
and there was a palm tree growing at the door which gave cocoanuts. There was a river where they got water and where they washed
and bathed. So though they were poor and had no house, they had
a good cave and a good time.

But when Chucho was a baby, his father died. So his mother took care of the corn-patch and they got along nicely, except one night while they were sleeping a mischievous monkey rolled a big rock to the door of the cave. In the morning, Chucho's mother could not get out because the rock was big and she was not strong enough to move it. Chucho was a baby so he could not do anything except blink, and when he saw his mother pushing so hard and crying, he cried too, waa-uhaaa—uhaaa! The monkey was up in the palm tree swinging by his tail.

Soon a mule-driver came by. Chucho's mother heard the mules drinking and splashing in the river and she heard the man talking to them, "Whoa, Whoa, Star of the Night! Whoa, Whoa, Morning Glory! Whoa, Whoa!" Those were the names of the mules. She called, "Help!" and the mule-driver came and saw the big rock and Chucho's mother trying to push. He could just see her head and hear her calling, "Help!" He came to help but the monkey swung up to the top of the palm tree and started throwing cocoanuts at him. Crack! There goes one, it nearly hit him. Zip! There goes another, and crack, crack, crack, some more, like cannon-balls. Some of them hit the mule-driver, but he came anyway and he rolled the rock away and Chucho's mother with baby Chucho in her arms climbed on one of the mules, the one named Morning Glory, and went to the town with the mule-driver.

After that they did not live in the cave any more. They stayed in town and Chucho's mother married the mule-driver and he took care of them. Sometimes he took Chucho along when he made trips with the mules, carrying packs of things from town to town, to sell in the market. Sometimes cocoanuts, sometimes pineapples, sometimes corn, sometimes pots, and sometimes birds in a crate. Parrots, for instance.

Chucho saw many things and when he was seven years old he was
a big boy and knew how to saddle and load the mules and how to
talk to them, "Whoa, Star of the Night! Ahrrrrrre! Ahrrrrrre,
Poppy! Arrrrrre, Diamond! Back up, Morning Glory!" He was
strong and knew how to go on errands because he was not afraid.
It just happened he did not know fear. Even the grown people
were surprised because they were afraid sometimes, but Chucho
wasn't. It was his destiny.

One day Chucho was going to the market to buy some brown
sugar and pink yarn for his mother. She needed these things. He
met Ignacio. Ignacio was a big boy, maybe fourteen years old, who
had a job. His job was to ring the bells of the church every morning and every evening. He had to climb up the stairs, long, long
narrow stairs to the top of the church where the bells were. "Good
morning, Ignacio, how are things with you?" asked Chucho.

"Not so good, Chucho, not so good."

"Why, what is the matter?"

"Something funny is going on in that church. People say one
thing, they say another, but all I know is that last night when I went
up to ring the bells I heard a moaning sound. Then I heard screaming, like a nahual. I ran down very fast but I'm sure something
tried to pull my hair. I'm going to the priest right now and tell him
I resign. I resign my job."

"Somebody must be hiding there," said Chucho.

"I think it's ghosts," said Ignacio. "I don't want a job with ghosts
in it. Or again it may be the priest. Maybe those things they say
about him are true, such as that he turns people into animals and
other funny things like that."

"Why don't you ask him?" said Chucho.

"Oh, no. They say if you ask him you disappear, you become a

116

bull or a calf or something. He makes cattle out of dead people, so they say. Oh, no, I wouldn't ask him."

"Let's do this," said Chucho. "You tell the priest you're very sick or something, and that I am going to ring the bells until you get well. There must be somebody hiding there. I have the intention of finding out."

"Aren't you afraid, Chucho?"

"Oh, I can take care of myself," he said. "I know a thing or two."

So they made that arrangement between them. That evening Chucho said to his mother, "I have something to attend to," and he went to the church. He slipped in very quietly, this was before time for ringing the bells, and he hid behind an altar.

Soon he heard moaning and screaming. It sounded like somebody hurt. "It must be a cat," said Chucho. But then he heard soft footsteps, slip slip slip, and he saw a man with a big knife. There was a woman too. They looked all around and then they began to rob. They took the jewels off the saints. They opened cupboards and they took gold cups out. They took silver candlesticks off the altars. They had a big sack and everything went into that. "Quick," said the woman. "I think I hear the priest coming."

"Oh, that's all right," said the man. "It's all fixed." And when the priest came, the man said, "Here is your part," and he gave him a bagful of gold coins.

The priest said, "Hurry, it is almost time for the bells to ring and the people to come and pray, and I have to fix everything so nobody will suspect anything. Hurry, maybe the boy who rings the bells will see you."

"Oh, that's all right," said the man with the knife. He rolled his eyes fiercely and said, "That's all fixed too. We will hide and you go up in the bell tower and when the boy comes to ring the bells,

117

scare him. Then he will not ring the bells and the people won't come to church so soon and we will run. We will be gone a good long way before anybody suspects anything. No one will catch us."

"All right." said the priest, "but hurry because I have a little business of my own to attend to. Some cows and things I have to look after."

The wicked priest went up the stairs to the bell-tower. He hid there. It was time to ring the bells, so Chucho slipped out and then opened the church door loudly and came in whistling. It was dark but he knew his way around so he went up the stairs. While he was going up he heard a long moan and then a scream. "Aha!" said Chucho. "That is the priest imitating ghosts and nahuals." So he moaned too. "Ooooowah, ooowah, ooooo!"

"That's peculiar," said the priest. "Where could that noise be coming from?" Then he moaned and howled. And Chucho howled too. "It must be an echo," said the priest, getting worried.

Now Chucho was at the top. He was reaching for the bell-rope when he heard a long, long howl right next to him. What did he do? He pretended he didn't hear and reached higher for the bell-rope. "How strange," thought the priest, and he howled louder. But Chucho reached the bell-rope and began to ring. Clang-clang! Bong! Bong! Bong-ding-dong-ding-bong! The people heard this and began getting ready to come to prayers.

"I must do something," said the priest. He reached out and pulled Chucho's hair. What did Chucho do? He pretended he didn't feel anything, just kept on ringing the bells. Bong-bong-bong-ding! Ding-Dong! He played a tune on them. The priest pulled his hair harder, and the harder he pulled, the harder Chucho rang the bells. Each time the priest pulled, Chucho played a loud tune on the bells.

"I am getting desperate," said the priest. "Everything will be spoiled by this foolish boy." So he leaned far over and pulled Chucho's hair. He held on to it and pulled hard and meanwhile he screamed in his ear. Chucho pulled the biggest bell up, up, up, then suddenly turned around and let it go. It came swinging down bonging and the priest could not get out of the way. The bell hit him bang, bong, and knocked him off the bell-tower and he fell off the church and broke. He broke into many pieces. Then he went up in smoke.

The people were coming to the church and they saw the priest fall and then go up in smoke. "So that's how it was," they said. "There was something strange about that priest after all. Too bad."

They went in to say their prayers. There was the big man with the big knife and the woman, and they had the sack of robbed things. They were trying to run but the things they were carrying were too heavy. So they were caught. They were put in jail. And Chucho came down from the bell-tower and said, "I guess I will go home now, I am a little tired," but the people clapped and clapped and said he was a hero. "How can I be a hero if the priest fell down all by himself?" said Chucho. So he went home.

After that, Florencio and Margarita and the others who had been turned into animals by the wicked priest became people again and went quietly home. Of course the dead people who had been turned into cattle just became dead people again. They went back to their graves, rolled themselves up in their mats and lay down in peace once more. Some people said, "Maybe Chucho isn't Chucho, maybe he is Tepozton," but when anybody mentioned that to Chucho he just laughed.

"How can I be Tepozton if I am Chucho?" he said.

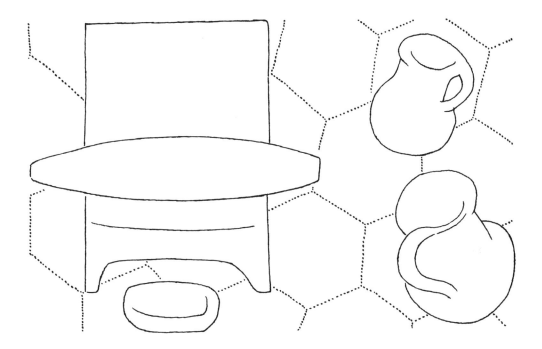

Maria Sat on the Fire

Once there was a girl named Maria. She worked in the house of some rich people. She was the cook. But she was very wasteful, very wasteful indeed. When she lighted the fire, she left it burning even when she was not cooking anything.

It is not right to waste fire or water or salt. It is wrong to throw food away too. Some people say that anybody who wastes food turns into an ugly animal when he dies. Other people say no, but he has to come back and pick it all up, instead of just resting nicely in his grave.

Maria worked in the rich man's house for ten years. Then she got sick and had to go home. And then she died. The lady of the house heard about it and said, "Isn't that too bad!"

A whole year later somebody knocked on the door of the house. And it was Maria. The lady of the house came to the door and Maria said to her, "Good morning, ma'am. How are you? How is everything?"

But the lady was surprised. She said, "Listen, Maria, aren't you dead?"

"Why yes, I am dead," said Maria. "Certainly I am dead. I am not alive at all. I just came to the door because God told me I had to work for you again, to punish me for being wasteful. So please do me the favor of letting me work for you. I promise that you won't have to pay me a cent. I just want to go to heaven."

Then the lady asked for an explanation and Maria said, "Well, you see it was because I did wrong. Do you remember how I used to make a big fire and just let it burn? And how I threw good food away? Now I have to make up for all that."

When the lady understood how it was, she had to take Maria back. Of course she had other servants too, and they all knew Maria and were very glad to see her again. But they were always wondering about her because she never ate anything. Nothing at all, ever. When they all sat down to supper she just waited on them, but didn't take anything herself.

At last one of them asked her, "Why don't you eat, Maria?"

"Why yes, I eat," she said. "I eat when I cook. Haven't you noticed?"

But they never saw her eat and they wondered and wondered. One night, just when everybody was getting ready to go to bed, the lady of the house asked, "What is Maria doing so late in the kitchen?"

"She must be putting the dishes away," they told her. It was nine o'clock and all the servants were getting ready for bed. Maria,

122

being the cook, had to put everything away. But when the kitchen was all cleaned up, she wiped the stove off neatly and sat down on it. There she sat with the fire burning under her.

And that is what the lady saw when she peeked. But she didn't say a word. She just thought it was very strange that Maria should sit on the fire.

The next day she invited the priest to come and have chocolate at her house. The priest was a wise man. The lady told him all about Maria.

"You mean she is dead?" said the priest.

"Why yes," said the lady. "Yes, she's dead."

"Well maybe she is dead," said the priest, "maybe she is. But I don't believe she would sit on the fire."

So he peeked too. And there was Maria, sitting on the burning coals. "That's very strange," said the priest. He walked into the kitchen. "Why are you sitting on the fire, Maria?"

"God told me to," she answered.

"Do you mean God?" said the priest.

"Why yes," said Maria. "He is very nice. Only I have to sit on the fire because when I was alive I used to waste it."

"Oh, I see," said the priest. "I see how it is. That's all right then." So he blessed her.

And the fire went out, and Maria disappeared. After that she never came back any more.

Malintzin

Malintzin was a person who could talk many languages. She was very lovely too. When the Spaniards came to Mexico she could talk to them, she could understand what they said. She told the Mexican kings and then she told the Spaniards the answers. She fell in love with Cortes, who was the chief of the Spaniards, so she persuaded the Mexican kings to give him everything. Everything. Gold and jewels and fine feathers and chocolate and all the best things in the land.

But the Spaniards were not satisfied with the gold and the presents. They never had enough, everybody knows how they are. They wanted more. They wanted to be the kings and to have everybody work for them so they could have more gold and more everything. Always more and more. The Mexican kings were not willing to agree to this. So the Spaniards put some of them in jail, and there were big battles. Many people were killed, many were tortured, to make them say where the treasures were. To make them give everything. When Malintzin saw this, she became very sad. She cried and cried until she died.

A wind came and carried her away to the top of a mountain. The name of this place is Texocotepec, that is, Hill Where the Tejocote Trees Grow. The trees give their little yellow fruits there. This mountain has fire inside. It gives off smoke and fire and melted rocks. There are many caves in it. Malintzin lives there and every night she cries. You can hear her. That is the crying you hear in the wind. She cries about all the terrible things that happened to the people. She pulls her long black hair.

She lives with the Nahuaques. They are the persons who make things grow. When they get angry you have to go and beg them not to be angry, because otherwise they won't send any rain, and if it doesn't rain nothing grows. Then comes the dry time. There is nothing green anywhere, nor anything to eat. But if you go creeping into the cave of a Nahuaque, you will see many little plants growing there. Squashes, and tomatoes, and baby corn. The thing to do is to tie bows of ribbon on these plants, red and white. The Nahuaques like bows of ribbon. They also like colored tissue paper, red and white. This pleases them and they send rain.

When they see the ribbons, the chief Nahuaque says to all the other Nahuaques, "Well, brothers, shall we eat?" They say, "Yes, sire, let us eat." They gather around him and they eat together.

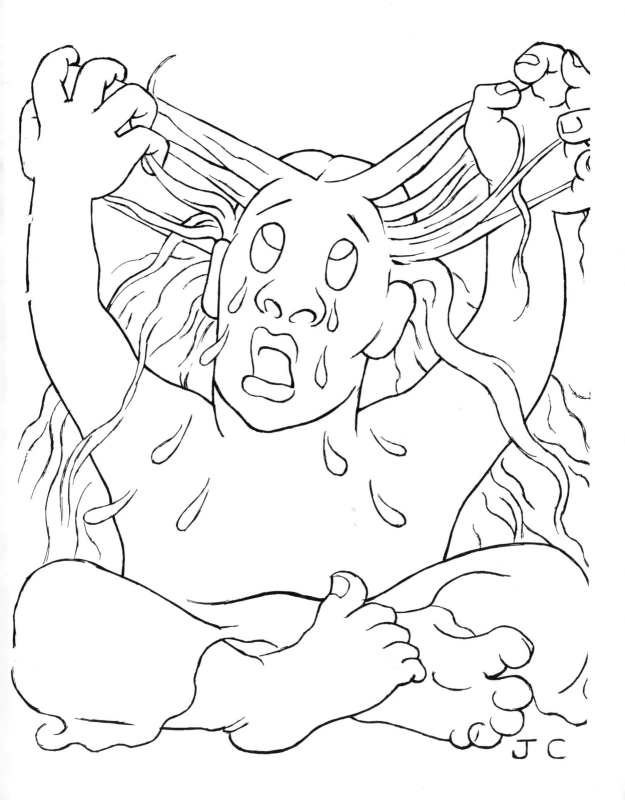

And everything that they eat, grows. But whatever they leave out dries up, or the worms get it. You can see it dying in the fields.

Well, Malintzin is enchanted there with the Nahuaques. Every day at twelve o'clock, when the sun is brightest, all light; bugles blow and drums are heard. Out comes Malintzin to warm herself in the sun. But at night she cries, pulling her long hair because she helped the white men and it turned out so badly.

They say that now she is a great big fat woman. Around her neck she wears many strings of beads, mostly corals, and some green jade. When there is a revolution the bugles blow very hard, and the drums beat twice as loud. Out marches Malintzin, leading a troop of soldiers. They fight the army which comes to hurt the people. But at night she cries because so many people die.

Once a general with many soldiers came to her mountain, where she is enchanted. He annoyed the people who live in the towns around there. He killed men and women and innocent little children. Then he went away, twisting his mustaches. Not far, though. A thunderbolt came down and there ended the general. The people came out. They saw a great big fat woman sitting where the lightning had struck. She was pulling her long hair and big tears fell on her bare feet. She cries when people die. You can hear it in the wind.

A Note on the Illustrations

This book was written fifty years ago. The stories in it are old, and were probably first heard by the storyteller, Luz, nearly 100 years ago. Luz (whose name means "light" in Spanish), lived in the Mexican village of Milpa Alta and she knew these stories well from her childhood. She told them to Anita Brenner, who wrote them down here.

Luz was a wonderful woman, and she was beautiful. She was not rich; she did not wear fancy clothes. She was an Indian, and she had long, black braids and a peaceful smile. When Luz was young, the country of Mexico was ruled by people who believed that the only things beautiful or worthwhile came from Europe. The art academy taught students to draw and paint like Europeans; architects copied the designs of the French or Italians, the Austrians or the Spanish; those who ruled even dressed in European clothes and spoke French!

This had been going on for 400 years and many of the Mexican people had had enough. They were tired of hiding their own religious and artistic traditions. They were tired of pretending to be European. They wanted to participate and rule themselves; they wanted to express their pride in being Mexican in an open way. So they elected a new president, and fought for ten years for a new constitution. There were bloody battles in this Mexican Revolution, but they finally won a new government, and with it, change.

Immediately the rich heritage of Mexico bloomed forth. Artists painted brown-skinned people who looked Mexican, not European. Festivals, and flowers, and the simple things of life filled their canvases with color. The imposing pyramids and beautiful pottery of the early Aztecs and Mayans became sources for new inspiration, and people drew, painted, and built freely in their own, Mexican style.

One day Luz met Jean Charlot, an artist born in France whose mother's family was from Mexico. Charlot had brought back to Mexico the fresco technique that the Mexican people had used many centuries before. He painted the first fresco mural in Mexico in modern times—and he drew the pictures in this book, as well as in many others. Charlot was one of the first artists to depict the Mexican people simply in their ordinary country dress. Today, of course, you won't find many people in Mexico who look the way these drawings do. Most Mexicans wear modern clothes. But Luz's forebears had fought hard to be themselves, and Jean Charlot had drawn them as themselves, not as other people had wished them to be.

Susannah Glusker
March 1992

About the Author

Anita Brenner was born in Aguascalientes, Mexico, in 1905. She grew up during the time of the Mexican Revolution, overhearing whispers of fighting at the dinner table, and departing suddenly for Texas when things got rough. Here Brenner attended school and some college before returning to Mexico in 1923.

Although Anita Brenner was scarcely eighteen years old, the path to her future was set. She taught, translated, and wrote, becoming part of the group of intellectuals and artists that included Jean Charlot, Tina Modolti, José Clemente Orozco, Diego Rivera, Edward Weston, and many others who today are considered the elite of the Mexican renaissance in the arts.

In 1927, Brenner moved to New York, where she completed her Ph.D. in anthropology at Columbia University, published her first book, and married Dr. David Glusker in 1930. They had two children. While her husband was in the army, she returned to Mexico where her best-known book, *The Wind That Swept Mexico*, was published in 1943.

Anita Brenner's children's books include *Dumb Juan and the Bandits*, *A Hero by Mistake*, and *The Timid Ghost*. She created and edited the publication "Mexico: This Month" for seventeen years, and contributed to major magazines and newspapers in the United States. Brenner also spent many hours farming the family land in Aguascalientes in her later years. She died in an automobile accident in Mexico, December 1974.

About the Illustrator

Jean Charlot was born in Paris in 1898. Known today as the master muralist of Mexico, Charlot actually did not go to Mexico until he was twenty-two—after service in World War I in North Africa. Fascinated with things Mexican from his boyhood experiences with an uncle's art and book collection, Charlot joined the circle of artists and thinkers who were creating a renascence in the Mexican arts in the 1920s.

Charlot was multi-talented as a muralist, a painter, a sculptor, writer, book illustrator, lecturer, teacher, and even archaeologist. The simple massive shapes of his style, and the gracefulness of his line, harked back to ancient Aztec and Mayan forms and were ideally suited to children's books. Charlot illustrated many in his long career, including several by Anita Brenner and Margaret Wise Brown.

Jean Charlot's work can be seen all over the United States and Mexico, and especially in Hawaii, where he finally settled. He died in 1979.